MORTON PUBLIC LIBRARY DISTRICT

A130

W9-CFV-341

YOUNG ADULT LEV
Levine, Anna
Freefall

AR 3.9
7 PTS

DISCARD

Freefall

Anna Levine

JUN   2011

MORTON PUBLIC LIBRARY DISTRICT
315 W. PERSHING
MORTON, ILLINOIS 61550

Greenwillow Books
An Imprint of HarperCollins Publishers

This book is a work of fiction. References to real people, events,
establishments, organizations, or locales are intended only to provide
a sense of authenticity, and are used to advance the fictional narrative.
All other characters, and all incidents and dialogue, are drawn from
the author's imagination and are not to be construed as real.

Freefall
Copyright © 2008 by Anna Levine

All rights reserved. No part of this book may be used or reproduced
in any manner whatsoever without written permission except in the
case of brief quotations embodied in critical articles and reviews.
Printed in the United States of America. For information address
HarperCollins Children's Books, a division of HarperCollins
Publishers, 1350 Avenue of the Americas, New York, NY 10019.
www.harperteen.com

The text of this book is set in Caslon.
Book design by Victoria Jamieson

Library of Congress Cataloging-in-Publication Data

Levine, Anna.
Freefall / by Anna Levine.
p. cm.
"Greenwillow Books."
Summary: As war between Israel and Lebanon breaks out in 2006
and her compulsory service in the Israeli army draws near, teenaged
Aggie considers joining an elite female combat unit.
ISBN: 978-0-06-157654-6 (trade bdg.)
ISBN: 978-0-06-157656-0 (lib. bdg.)
[1. Self-realization—Fiction. 2. Soldiers—Fiction.
3. Israel—Fiction. 4. Lebanon War, 2006—Fiction.] I. Title.
PZ7.L57823Fr 2008 [Fic]—dc22 2008003826

First Edition 10 9 8 7 6 5 4 3 2 1

Greenwillow Books

To my sons, Nimrod and Tomer, and their friends
Aviran, Raz, Omri, Nir, Ido, Amit, Ariel, and Yossef.
And to Danielle and Ayla. Thank you all
for your help and inspiration.

A special thanks to
Randi Firpo Hanegbi, writer and friend,
and to my agent, Rosemary Stimola

And always, for Alex

I am about to jump.

I am about to jump wearing a full load on my back.

Feet, knees, hip, back, roll.

Crammed tightly, the pack is stuffed with my anxieties, fears—and the army-issued parachute. It is secured to my chest with strings and clasps. It holds my heart in place, should it try to break free. When the time is right, I will yank the cord.

At that moment, the pack will open. My fears will rise to the dome of my chute, where they will hover. And for a moment, I will be free of them.

Feet, knees, hip, back, roll. I have been trained to react without thinking. My body knows the drill. I will fall. Drift. Soar. Once my feet make contact with the ground, I will drop to my knees, lean into my hip, flip onto my back, and roll.

Not another rehearsal; this is reality. Am I ready? Yes. I can do this. Really, I can.

The door is pushed open. A rush of air blasts at me. The noise of the airplane motor swells and crashes inside my head.

I am sandwiched in. We shuffle forward like penguins. Birds without wings forced to fly. My hands clench the rungs. I have been trained for this moment, but nothing can tame the terror in my bones and the fear churning in my stomach. My thoughts rush around. What if—

"Green!"

I'm not ready to let go.

"Jump!"

I can't. The air batters against my chest, pressing me back. The engine thunders in my head. There's nothing out there—but an empty void. My fingers are pried from the rungs.

"Holy—"

My hands are wrenched free.

"Oh no—I'm not—"

A shove on my back.

"Wait—I—"

Feet, feet . . . knees . . . hip?

Chapter One

I jump into the taxi.

Shira follows behind me. Ben and Ron hop in through the opposite door.

"It's so cold out there," says Shira.

"And it's supposed to be spring." I scoot to the middle and snuggle next to Ben. The spaghetti-strap top I thought perfect earlier in the evening does little to keep out the cold. "We shouldn't have worn skirts," I say to Shira, my teeth chattering.

"Better?" asks the taxi driver, turning up the heater.

"Getting there," I say, rubbing my knees.

The driver looks us over in the rearview mirror. "Four separate drop-offs will cost you extra."

"Come on," says Ben. "We're all in the same area."

He revs the motor but doesn't drive.

"I'll get off with Shira," Ron offers.

The taxi driver shifts into gear and takes off down King George, honking and swearing at everything that moves.

"Rush hour. You'd think it was five in the afternoon, not midnight."

Midnight on a Thursday and the town is packed with people trying to grab parking spots closest to the bars.

The driver careens through the narrow streets. I am thrown against Ben with each tight swerve. Finally the taxi pulls to a stop in front of Shira's house.

"Your mom's at the window," says Ron.

"As usual." Shira jumps out and blows us all a kiss. "G'night!" she shouts. "And good luck, Ben. Next week, my house. We'll celebrate."

Ron leans through the taxi window. "Okay, Ben. Show 'em how it's done. Call me as soon as you get back."

"You bet."

We watch as Ron waits for Shira to run up the stairs, and then he darts behind her house, where he disappears into the maze of alleyways that crisscross through the courtyards.

Ben glances at his watch.

"Nervous?" I ask.

He shrugs. "I think it'll be okay. They said we had to have at least eight hours of sleep before the exercise or we're immediately disqualified, which would mean waiting another month until the next trial."

"Maybe you shouldn't have gone out with us tonight?"

"Probably, but my dad was driving me crazy."

I wait for him to go on. We're at a traffic light, and now that I've warmed up, I'm in no hurry to get home. We're still sandwiched together though Ron and Shira are gone and there's room to spread out. I rest my head against his shoulder.

"You should have heard him," says Ben. "It was painful. 'In my day, pre-army training courses were tough.'" Ben mimics his father's gravelly voice. "'Keep away from the slackers, son. You don't want them to think you're a shirker. Grab the stretcher and leave the lighter loads for the wimps.'" Ben shakes his head. "If I don't make it—"

I hear the catch in his throat and nudge him in the ribs with my elbow. "Since when have you ever doubted yourself?" I tease him. "You've been training for this since junior high. Look at those biceps." I give his arm a playful squeeze.

He laughs. "You're right. I've just got to stay focused."

The taxi draws up in front of my place. The flicker of the TV screen shines through the curtain slits. "My dad's still awake."

"The late-night news?"

"Of course. They interviewed him this morning, and he keeps watching the reruns."

"Like living with a movie star."

"Oh, please." I groan. "When was the last time you saw a Knesset minister on the cover of *People* magazine?"

The taxi driver laughs. He looks at us through the rearview mirror. "In this country," he says, "everybody's got to be a somebody."

"Tell me about it," says Ben.

Before opening the door I turn toward Ben for our familiar cheek-peck good-bye. But this time something more happens. Maybe the taxi jolts or maybe—I don't know—maybe we've both been waiting for the opportunity, but it's our lips that touch and for a moment, or longer, our bodies press together. His lips hold mine. His hand circles my waist.

I am suspended. My heart beats like tiny bird wings, and I hover in this unfamiliar territory before pulling away. I fumble out of the taxi and manage a breathless good-night. By the time I run down the path to the entrance of my building, there is only a glimmer of taillights left to remind me of the moment.

A week has passed since then.

I speed up, taking a shortcut toward Shira's house, urged on by the crispness in the air and the anticipation of seeing Ben again. Tonight not even the tantalizing aroma of falafel and freshly baked pita from the outdoor snack bars can tempt me to linger.

Cutting through the cherry tree garden, I skirt the gang of stray cats huddled for warmth outside the old synagogue and arrive almost breathless at Shira's house. Their iron gate, which borders the alley, is half open. As I step inside their garden, I notice Shira's brother sitting at the top of the stairs leading to the entrance to their house.

"Look, Noah, snowflakes!" Tilting my head to the sky, I watch them parachute their way down, covering the wet Jerusalem courtyard with a layer of white.

He watches me from beneath the porch awning and laughs. He's dressed in his army pants and a green thermal shirt with the sleeves rolled up to his elbows. A scruffy pair of reddish brown army boots are beside him. One of his thick socks has a hole where his toe pokes through. Traces of snow in his short-cropped hair hint that he too must have been looking up at the flakes just seconds earlier.

I run up the stairs, and he moves aside to let me pass.

"Aren't you coming in to see the game?"

"No. Got to go back to my base soon. I'd rather catch some peace and quiet out here." He reaches for his guitar, which is propped against the door. "Besides, I love the smell of snow."

"Me too." I glance back. "But Shira's waiting for me. I'll let you know how many baskets we're up at halftime," I promise, letting the screen door swing shut behind me as I step inside.

The house greets me with smells of Yemenite spices: coriander and some others I can't name. A plate of leftover *malawah* is on the counter. I'm hoping that Shira will ask me later if I want to take some home with me.

"I've saved this for you," says Dalia. Shira's mom points to the plate. "Pick it up on your way out."

"Thank you."

"A pleasure. The gang is in the den."

I toss my shoes onto the pile. Part of me would rather sit outside with Noah watching the snow fall, but before I can change my mind, Shira comes flying into the hall.

"Aggie! What took you so long to get here? I'm bursting with news!"

Her hug envelops me in a garden of jasmine blossoms.

"Well, how did it go?"

"Amazing!" She flashes me a glossy purple smile. "Totally amazing. My first audition! With all those military personnel watching me, I thought my voice would crack, but I sang like honey!"

"And? You made it?"

"Really, Aggie." She fans her fingers through her thick hair. Yemenite hair. Full of decisive, tight dark curls. "They don't tell you right away! Total chaos would erupt. World War Three. The competition is more explosive than a minefield." She licks her lips and glances over my shoulder, examining herself in the hall mirror. Scowling, she moves closer to inspect an invisible blemish. "You should have seen some of the other girls looking at me. You'd think I was the enemy." She wipes away a smudge of mascara.

I check the mirror to see if the snow has made my makeup run.

"You know," she says, "with your coloring, you should use black eyeliner. It would make the blue in your eyes stand out more. Make them look smokier and less innocent."

"You think so?"

We stare at our faces in the mirror. Shira's dark eyes are so much more seductive than mine. Her hair is crammed into a bright purple hair band. My hair never stays put. It frizzes into a thousand confused directions in an uncommitted shade of light brown.

Shira sighs. "Anyway. 'Me?' I said to them. I said, 'We're all on the same side, you know. In the end, we'll all be wearing the same uniform and singing for the same troops.'"

"Except that some of you won't be. Some of you won't be chosen."

She spits three times, pursing her lips the way her grandmother has taught her, to ward off the evil eye. "You shouldn't say things like that! I hope you didn't jinx me."

"I meant the others, not you."

We look at each other in the mirror.

"Will we still have time for each other next year?" I ask. "You'll be off singing to the troops in some glamorous spot—and me?"

Shira turns and throws her arms around me. "And you, Aggie, will always be a major part of my life. You ground me." Holding me at arm's length, she says, "Without you I'd never see the stuff that matters. Songs would be melodies without meaning." She tugs on the end of my hair, and laughs. "We'll always be friends, no matter where you end up."

"That's exactly what I'm worried about. Where will I end up? What if they stick me somewhere I hate? Two years is a long time to be stuck behind some army desk. I'll go crazy filing papers, making coffee, and sitting in a stuffy room with a bunch of girls who probably have pop jingles for their ring tones."

Shira groans. "Don't be such a pessimist. You never know, your commanding officer might be a gorgeous hunk who will fall madly in love with you."

I shove her aside and make my way into the den. It's total chaos in there. The TV is on at full volume. The hollers and groans of the Maccabi game compete with the Shark girls singing from the stereo. Ben sits on the sofa cracking sunflower seeds and dropping the shells into a bowl balanced on his thigh while he shouts above it all, telling Ron about the field exercise.

"Then he said, 'Fill it up, all the way up!' In the end the sandbags weighed, oh man, at least twenty-five kilo."

Shira grabs my arm. Her sigh drowns out the coach's

call of foul as even Ben stops to look up. The blood rushes to my face. Ben notices. Winks. I see him nudge Ron in the ribs and whisper something.

"I'm so wired, Aggie. Getting into the army's entertainment corps is like—is like making the charts before you've made your first single."

"'Forty seconds,' our commander shouts. 'Run! Up the hill and back.'"

"With the sacks?" Ron puts his beer on the edge of the table and leans in closer to Ben.

"Rebound!"

Ben stands to turn up the volume on the TV and catches my eye before he sits back down. He looks thinner. His jeans hang lower on his waist, but from the sound of his voice and the look on his face, he's made it through the first round. Half listening to Shira, I strain to catch Ben's conversation. "He kept shouting, 'Quit now if you can't hack it.'"

"My voice never wavered," says Shira.

"'Again!' he shouts. 'That wasn't forty seconds. Now do it in thirty-five.'"

"*I have no other country*," Shira belts out.

"No way. Thirty-five seconds?" Ron's beer teeters on the edge of the table.

"Yeah," says Ben. "And we had to shout out each second as it passed. Thirty more times. The hill. Back. Hill. Back. Then, my luck, the strap on my back broke! I had to carry the sack in my arms like a fat calf." He rolls up his sleeves to show the cuts and bruises—and his solid muscles. "My arms were killing me. Some of the guys tried spilling out sand while the commander wasn't looking. As if a cupful would make a difference."

"And then—"

"Then when I got on stage"—Shira pauses to smooth back her hair—"all the nervousness disappeared. You know that feeling? Aggie, you know what I mean?"

"What a move! Stellar defense by Israel's Maccabi team."

"Hey, Shira, can you put on some normal music?" asks Ron. "Their voices are driving me nuts. We can't hear the game."

"It's *West Side Story*—and get used to it. I'm practicing for an audition."

I nod as if I'm with her on stage, but I am with Ben in the desert, a bag of sand heavy in my arms as I run back and forth thirty times. I feel sweaty. My shoulders ache. My legs, as if cased in concrete, are too heavy to lift. I lean against the table.

"'No slacking. Get moving!' He kept shouting for us to hurry up. Taunting us that we didn't have what it takes. It was the dead of night. We were walking with canteens, ammo round our waists, an M16 and all our stuff on our backs. And he's striding along expecting us to keep up. There wasn't even a ray of moonlight. At first we walked with him, but then the gap kept getting wider. 'Keep up!' he shouted."

"And?" Ron prompts him.

"There was no way—"

"I'll die if I don't get in." Shira's voice quivers. "If I don't get in, then I'm not going. No one can make me do what I don't want to do. Are you listening, Aggie?"

She shakes my arm. I focus on the colored stud in her right nostril. This one's a garnet. It catches the light and reflects it back at me. I think of the stars. Ben in the desert, the darkness, the sounds of boots crushing the earth and the burdened breaths of the group as, exhausted, they push on.

"You can't tell them you aren't going," I say to Shira. "That's kind of the definition of compulsory service: you don't have a choice."

"You girls have it easy," says Ron. "Two years of service is nothing next to our three."

"Did you hear about Micha?" says Ben. "Made the pilot's course. Had to sign on for seven years."

"No way! I sweated through those exams but got bounced out faster than a whirling propeller. Man, they were tough." Ron balances the beer bottle on his knee. "I've got my field test for paratroopers next week. It'll be a breeze in comparison." He puts his hands over his ears. "And shut off the music, will you, Shira?"

Shira shudders. "If they think I'll sit in an office for two years, they can forget it! This is my future career we're talking about!"

"What are you going to do?" I ask her.

"—go *to live in Amer-i-ca*," she sings together with the Shark girls.

I shake my head and roll my eyes. "You'd be lost there without us."

She smothers me in a cloud of jasmine. "Teasing. I would never leave you guys. I would never leave—"

"Pure agony." Ben groans. "Then he told us to put the sacks on the stretchers. My shoulder, see the cuts?"

He rolls down the collar of his shirt and shows off the deep gash along his shoulder.

"Hey, getting into an entertainment troop is just as tough as getting into one of your elite units," says Shira.

She leans over to reach for some sunflower seeds.

Ben stops midsentence. He's distracted. It's not Maccabi's main player scoring, the Shark girls singing, the commander's shouts, or even me. It's Shira's silver Star of David, which swivels seductively above the sunflower seed dish. Like a spelunker caught in a narrow cavern, Ben is lost inside a maze of cleavage.

Shira straightens up. She catches Ben ogling, and giggles.

"We're in the lead by seventeen!" shouts Ron.

"Triple double! Triple double. Come on, Tal."

Shira dives for the spot on the floor in front of the TV. Behind her, on the worn, black leather couch, Ben and Ron sit side-by-side. Shira's head is close enough to rest on Ben's knee should he scoot up behind her. It should be my spot. I try and catch Ben's attention, but he is leaning forward, his body rigid as our offense gets the ball and heads down the court.

I hesitate. I'm sure Shira doesn't mean anything by it. But I feel benched, watching from the sidelines. Surprised and winded.

Maybe what happened in the taxi was just my imagination—or maybe now I was only imagining the way he looked at Shira.

It's the beginning of the second quarter. I listen to the squeal of running shoes, watch the flash of yellow jerseys as our players spin and dash around the court determined to hold on to their advantage.

"Win or die! Win or die!" Ben hollers.

"Hey, Aggie," says Shira. "Can you bring in some more beers?"

"Sure," I say, deciding to make light of it.

As I head for the kitchen, I hear strums of an old Dylan refrain drift in off the porch. Noah is still playing. Peeking outside, I see it's stopped snowing. I feel cheated that I've missed it. Maybe the only snowfall Jerusalem will have all year. Easing open the screen door made for flies in the summertime and not this winter's cold, I step out onto the porch. A scooter screeches down the narrow alley and stops below the house.

"Hey, Noah. How's it going?" yells the driver.

"Okay and you?"

He revs the motor in reply. "You're going back?"

"Yeah. I'm closing this weekend."

"Too bad. There's a party by the port in Tel Aviv tomorrow. Next time," he calls over his shoulder as he speeds off.

Noah continues strumming on his guitar as he looks

up at me. He's got his dad's light hazel-colored eyes and his mom's tanned complexion. He is a perfect meld of east and west. "*For the times they are a-changin',*" he sings in a voice that's deeper and rougher than Shira's but just as strong.

I hover by the doorway. He hasn't asked me to join him but hasn't turned his back on me either.

"Not a basketball fan after all?" he asks me.

"Win or die! Win or die!" The rousing chorus from inside spills onto the porch.

"Shame to miss the snowfall," I say. "Maybe the only one we'll have for the next couple of years."

Leaning back, his guitar resting on his thigh and his head cocked to the side, he'd look like a hippie if it weren't for the army uniform and military haircut. He's wearing his boots, and sometime between when I said hi and now, he's polished them and packed up. The duffel bag lies by his foot like a faithful pet. His M16 is propped on the banister. I'm still leaning against the door, catching Shira's giggle followed by Ben's muffled reply.

"I wish I knew what I wanted." I sigh. "Shira's lucky she's so talented. She's perfect for the entertainment troop. I'm sure she'll get in."

He picks a few bars of a new song then pauses. "You can't know what you want until you can't have it."

"Are those Dylan lyrics?"

"Not exactly." He reaches for his guitar case. "When something slips out of your grasp and you realize it's gone, that's when it hits you. If it's something you didn't want anyway, you'll let it go. If it's what you want, you'll do whatever it takes to get it back."

I glance over my shoulder wondering about Ben. Would I do whatever it takes to get him if Shira decides she wants him—or he decides he wants her?

Noah pushes the cuffs of his army pants into his boots. I watch as he threads the laces all the way up and ties the ends in a knot. He takes care to smooth down his pants and wipe off a smudge of dirt from his heel.

"So what is it you want?" I ask him.

Standing up, he swings his rifle over his shoulder. "Peace and quiet. Space. Time to play my guitar. Read. Think."

I glance at the army bag by his feet. "Exactly what you don't have now?"

He smirks. "Not when you're sharing your tent with a bunch of other guys." He swings his guitar over his other shoulder and grabs his duffel bag. "I've got to walk over to the bus stop. You should go back inside. See who's winning."

He means the basketball game. I'm thinking of Shira, Ben, and me. I realize I'm not interested in the games going on inside the den. I'd rather talk to Noah.

"Actually," I say, "the bus stop is on my way home. I'll walk with you. I was planning on leaving anyway."

"Without your shoes?" He glances at my feet.

I'm still in my socks. "Right." I run back in and lace up my shoes in less time than it took him. I dash out only to find that somehow Noah's mom has made it out before me. She stands on her tiptoes, her arms wrapped around his neck, reaching up to kiss him as he bends to hug her.

I stop—feeling a lump in my throat as if the air I'm breathing has become infused with a tenderness so potent it's contagious.

"Call me as soon as you can," she says.

"Yes, Mom."

"Tell your commander I want you home next weekend. We're having a birthday party for Grandma."

He laughs. "Oh sure, he'll go for that. Anything else?"

"You need to have more time to rest." She hands him a bag of cookies. "They just came out of the oven."

He takes a deep breath and sighs. "Delicious. The guys are going to love them." He catches me watching, smiles, shrugs, and blushes.

"And I packed you some extra boxers and—"

"Mom."

"Oh, all right." She sighs and turns around, her shoulders drooping inward. "And this is for you, Aggie." She gives me a paper bag spotted with oil stains. It's the *malawah*.

"Thank you," I say, pretending not to notice her tears.

"How did she know I was leaving?" I ask Noah as she walks back up the stairs into the house.

"Nothing gets by her."

We wave good-bye and start walking down the alley. The familiar refrains of the news broadcasts chime the hour from almost every house. Later the streets will fill with restaurant-goers, bar hoppers, and kids crowding the sidewalks mingling with friends.

For now the alleyways are empty except for me and Noah and patches of snow. We walk side-by-side, listening to the sound of our footsteps on the cobblestones. As we turn the corner, he waits for me to walk in front of him down a narrow passage where we must squeeze past a row of cars crowding up the sidewalk.

"This is probably the only place in the world where cars get the sidewalk and people use the road."

I giggle, listening to myself and feeling so young and stupid.

As he draws up again beside me, an awkward silence takes over. I never used to feel tongue-tied around him. But there's something different in the way he's acting with me. And the way he looks at me. His hint of a dimple in each cheek makes me want to try harder, sound smarter, act older.

We leave behind the narrow streets and reach the main intersection, where cars, buses, and taxis jostle for space. Noah stops at the corner. He doesn't seem hurried so we wait for the light to change. I force myself to get up the nerve to say something.

"I've got my three-hundred test coming up at the recruitment center," I blurt out.

"That's nothing to worry about," he says.

"Three hundred questions! I'll probably run out of answers after the first page." My voice rises. "I'll be the only recruit who has ever failed a personality test. They won't know what to do with me."

Noah laughs. The light turns green. He steps off the sidewalk with such grace. He seems unaware of the weights on him: the rifle knocking against his leg with every step, his guitar slung over his back, and his bulky duffel bag that makes it feel like he's leaving home forever.

"Only three hundred questions?" he says, turning to flash me a smile.

My house is straight up the next street, but I turn toward the bus depot with him. The station is slowly filling with other soldiers weighed down with rifles of their own, as well as heavy coats slung over their packs as if here they don't feel the cold. We stop before we reach the others.

"Why, 'only'?" I ask him.

"I can think of a thousand questions to ask you."

Curiosity gets the better of me. "Like what?"

"Like where was your favorite sunrise?" he asks without a moment's hesitation.

I scowl and am about to say how the army doesn't care about that kind of thing, but then I grab his arm and pull his sleeve. "I actually know the answer to that."

"I knew you would." His look encourages me to go on.

"It was at my aunt's—up north, near the sea. We got up early to go hiking. And it was the most amazing sight. At first the light crept over the hills, and then slowly the sky changed to red and orange. . . ." My voice trails off.

He tosses his bag on the ground and rests his guitar beside it. The gun stays strapped to him. He's smiling. I wonder if he's teasing me.

"Wait a second, there's no way they'd ask anything like that. It's a multiple-choice questionnaire. What kind of a question is that anyway?"

"The only kind I like. A question that reveals more than the obvious. First, you had a great answer."

I blush. "Just a fluke."

He shakes his head. "I've always noticed that about you. You see things that a lot of other people don't." He picks up his bag as if aware of some cue I've missed. "Most of Shira's friends wouldn't have had any idea."

I want to assure him that I am nothing like a lot of Shira's friends, but the army transport pulls up. There is a commotion of kisses, hugs, and duffel bags being thrown into the belly of the bus.

I stand awkwardly. I don't belong in this crowd that's being left behind, and yet, just like them with their own soldiers, I wish Noah didn't have to go yet. Our conversation has just started. There are more things I want to ask him—and want him to ask me. We've never had time alone together.

"When will you be back?"

"On leave?" He frowns. "Two weeks. When will I be back as a civilian? Another year."

As I'm standing with my arms across my chest to keep warm, Noah leans over and slides his hand around my waist. I tilt my head up, surprised by this move—and definitely not expecting what follows.

The touch of his lips on mine sends a shiver right through me.

"You'll do fine," he says. "Just be yourself, Abigail Jacobs." He hops onto the bus, then turns. "You've got nothing to be worried about."

"Thanks." My voice is barely above a whisper. My heart is thumping so hard I can't catch my breath.

What just happened? Did he just kiss me? Just a kiss? Or *kiss* kiss me.

The bus takes off, and I am left standing there feeling dizzy. He's Shira's brother, I need to remember. But I wish—I wish we had more time. You can't just leave me like this! I want to scream. What am I supposed to think? I've always known him, but now it's like he's someone else.

I search the sky. Will somebody please explain what's going on? Last month the possibility of having a boyfriend was about as likely as a March snowfall in Jerusalem.

Now not only has it snowed, but I've been kissed twice—and by two different guys.

Chapter Two

There are about a hundred of us sitting in this small and stuffy room, waiting while the army officers pass out the exam. The room is sparse— empty of all hints of personality. The walls aren't even white but more like hospital gray. There's nothing on them, either, nothing to catch your eye and let your mind daydream while thoughts sort themselves out. One row of windows, too high off the ground to give a view of grass or trees, allows some natural light to enter. I catch a glimpse of limitless blue sky with not even a cloud or a leftover snowflake to break the monotony.

One hundred of us—and not a sound is heard except the rustle of paper and the occasional nervous cough. No one dares, doesn't even consider sneaking a peek at the paper to the right or left.

Do you like cheese? Yes.

Have you ever cheated on a test? No.

Do you like bonfires? Yes.

Do you like cold drinks? No.

Have you ever told a lie? Yes.

Have you ever been in a fight? Yes.

Do you like coffee? Yes. No. Sometimes?

Have you ever had an out-of-body experience? Huh?

After two hundred of these I'm not sure of anything. Do I really like taking baths better than showers? And what are they going to think about me if I do?

But I keep going.

Has anyone ever given you an answer on a test?

Didn't I just answer that?

I wish I knew what they were looking for so I could give them the answers they want. But though I've decided that I want to get into a combat unit, it doesn't mean that the army wants me. The questions seem absurd. There must be some hidden logic behind them. At least that's what everyone says.

In a daze after three hours, I find myself back on the street. Tel Aviv is too loud and bustling. Grabbing a drink and a cheese pastry at the central station, I board the intercity bus. Of course there are no seats left. I settle down on the floor in the aisle sandwiched between two soldiers and facing the knees of a religious woman. Her skirt reaches her ankles and a book of psalms rests on her lap. As the tension inside me recedes, I doze off, only to wake up as the bus shifts gear for the climb up to Jerusalem.

Back home I sneak into my room, hoping to avoid another set of three hundred questions from Mom. Crawling into bed, I sleep twenty-four hours straight, getting up only to cram in a few hours of math in preparation for my finals next week.

But studying for exams seems irrelevant. What did Noah mean by having a thousand questions to ask me? What will they think of my three-hundred test? Did I pass? Can you fail? Should I have been so honest? I try to recall my answers, but my brain has reached full capacity, crammed with formulas for mathematical theories and solutions to problems of logic.

I open the window. The aromas drifting out of every house on the street mingle together, creating a pot luck stew. Hot, spicy, and sweet.

"Allo, Aggie. How's it going?"

I wave to Mom's friend Shula, who is out walking Benz. "Fine."

"When's your draft date?" she shouts over Benz, who is yelping at one of the stray cats.

"August."

"What will I do without you around to walk Benz?"

I shrug, though I know she's already spoken to our downstairs neighbor.

"Shabbat shalom." She waves and tugs Benz to follow.

"Shabbat shalom." I pull my head back inside, where the aromas of roast chicken, mushrooms, and rice fill the house. I'm hoping for brownies for dessert.

No one at home has interrogated me yet. The unasked questions are even worse because the answers are not multiple choice—more like full-length essays.

At precisely 6:57, the sound of Grandma's sensible shoes marching up to our second-floor apartment echo in the hallway.

"Ready for lineup?" my sister, Hila, calls as she passes my room.

I reach the door first, before Grandma knocks a second time. "Abigail darling!" She kisses my cheek. "You've got rings under your eyes. You need to get out and get more exercise. Where's your sister?"

"Hi, Grandma." Hila appears by my side.

"Put this on the table, will you, angel?" She hands Hila a Pyrex dish covered with a checked dish towel. "Where's your mother?"

"In the kitchen, Tzillah. I'm just warming up the potatoes in the oven. I'll be out in a minute."

"Don't rush, Eve. I'll find Aaron."

"In here, Mother." Dad is in the living room, which adjoins the dining area. He sits on the couch surrounded by piles of newspapers while he listens to the news commentators on the TV.

"At ease," Hila whispers in my ear as we follow Grandma into the living room. I can't help giggling.

"Girls," Dad says.

"Leave them be, Aaron. They're teasing me. Did you hear that radio interview on the army channel today?" she asks, pushing aside the papers to sit.

"Which one?"

"Enough news, please." Mom puts the salad in the center of the table. "Come eat. And can we at least turn the TV off on Friday night?" She straightens the challah cover while reaching for the remote that Dad has placed beside his fork.

"After the headlines, Eve." Dad snatches it up. "I'll put it on mute."

Dad sets the remote back by his fork, daring her to reach for it. He's faster at the draw, and she knows it. Mom flicks open her napkin and covers her lap.

"It's Friday night," she says, "and it would be nice to have a quiet Shabbat meal together."

"There's been fighting on the border," says Dad, glancing between her and the TV screen. "Tensions are high, and in my position I need to know what's going on in real time."

"Quite right," Mom says. "But even a minister of the Knesset should be able to eat a quiet dinner with his family once a week."

We all glance at the set. The reporter, a cute guy with spunky eyebrows, is pointing to a map of the Middle East. I am familiar with this scene replayed in different variations whenever threats flare on any of our borders or a new land-for-peace proposal is brought up and we are reminded of how little there is left to share.

"If not for me, at least do it for Hila," says Mom, looking at my sister, who is making an admirable attempt at keeping out of the argument. "You know she's trying to observe the Sabbath, and you're not making it any easier."

Dad puts the TV on mute.

Hila winces, opens her mouth, and shuts it. "Thanks, Dad," she says.

We exchange glances. Dad doesn't get the religious stuff, and Hila has given up trying to explain how it works.

"More wine, Mother?" asks Dad, holding the bottle over Grandma's glass.

"Why don't you leave the bottle right here." Grandma swirls the liquid and holds it up to the light. *"L'Chaim."*

"L'Chaim," we reply.

"Pass that stuff over here. This dish is wonderful, Eve," says Dad. "You've never made it before."

Holding it at arm's length, I pass Dad the dish of couscous covered in a thick, red tomato paste and dotted with bright orange carrots. Just a whiff of the hot peppers and my eyes start to water.

"What's in it?" asks Dad.

"Don't know," says Mom. "Your mother brought it. Did you make it, Tzillah, or pick it up somewhere? I didn't know you were so familiar with such unusual spices."

"Whew, it's hot in here." Dad stretches the collar of his shirt. "How long have the radiators been on, all afternoon?"

"No, dear, just for an hour or so. Aggie, pass your father a serviette. I think it's the mix of spices in your mother's dish. What is this, Tzillah, a Moroccan hot pepper?" Mom dangles the offending bit in the air.

Hila catches my eye.

"Steamed couscous, tomato *madbuha*, spiced carrots. My neighbor is Moroccan. She says hot spices are good for the digestion. She's eighty-nine years old and doesn't look like she's going anywhere too soon, if you know what I mean."

"I love Moroccan food," says Hila. "It's so . . . authentic."

Mom looks at her, opens her mouth, and shuts it.

"More wine anyone?" asks Grandma.

"I think the rest of us have had enough, but you go ahead."

"Thank you. I will. I love this Golan wine. Reminds me of the year I worked up north on kibbutz picking grapes. That was a time I'll never forget—"

Distracted, she glances at the growing red splotch on the tablecloth. "Oh blast, what a shame. Sorry, Eve."

"Don't worry about it. It's just a drop," says Mom. "It comes right out in the wash; it always does."

I toss my napkin over the stain. Grandma smiles at

me. "Aggie, you haven't touched your food. What's the army going to do with a scarecrow?"

"Not everyone has to be built like a paratrooper to serve," says Mom. "Right, Aggie?"

"Well—"

"I didn't say that, Eve. I was just wondering what Aggie is planning to ask for. Two years is a long time to be pushing papers in a stuffy office somewhere on a dingy army base." Grandma pushes back her chair until it reaches the edge of Mom's rollaway desk. She sets her wineglass on one of the piles of papers behind her.

"Oh, it's a bit early to start thinking about all of that," says Mom. "And besides, it depends on which papers you're pushing. Speaking of which, would you mind moving your wineglass, Tzillah? Those are my students' essays, and the pile isn't very sturdy." She sighs. "We could use more room in this house."

Hila pushes away her plate. "There are other ways to serve, you know. There's a lot a girl can do for the country. Look at me. If it weren't for people like me and the other girls I'm with who are doing national service within the hospitals and the development towns this whole country would collapse."

Grandma scoots her chair back to the table, reaches

out her hand, and places it over Hila's. "I didn't mean that as a criticism."

Hila's cheeks flush. "Sorry, Grandma. I know. It's just that—I—" She sighs. "Nobody seems to understand me. And everything is such a struggle."

"Life's a struggle," says Grandma. She swirls her wine. "Life." She lets loose a raspy smoker's chuckle. "It comes with no instruction manual, no guarantee, and a limited warranty. But we take it anyway and try to make the best of it." She reaches for Hila again. "I'm not putting down what you do or how you do it," says Grandma. "But besides nurse's and teacher's aides, we need a few people on the front lines. Right, Aggie? My neighbor's daughter got into a combat unit. How about it?"

"Well, I—"

"I think Aggie needs to decide for herself," says Mom. "She still has time. Still has finals to finish up. And let's not forget that she's not built like a John Deere tractor. She's built like me."

"True," says Grandma. "She is built like you were— once—but that doesn't mean she can't hold a gun."

"A gun!" Hila's eyes open so wide her pupils disappear. "They don't make short-barreled M16s short enough."

"Can someone pass the chicken?" asks Dad.

"I thought you were cutting down," says Mom.

"Bravo, Mom!" says Hila. "As Minister of Agriculture Dad should be concerned about the way chickens are abused. If people were to eat less meat altogether—"

"We eat meat only occasionally, Hila. I think you can let your father enjoy his food without turning it into a national issue. I was just pointing out that he has to start watching his calorie intake."

Hila rests her hands on her lap. "Sorry, Dad."

"Rachel's daughter, the fat one, just got back from Hebron." Grandma pours herself another glass of wine. "She's serving in some godforsaken outpost. She says it's freezing cold but she wouldn't want to be anywhere else." She swirls the wine before taking a long sip. "She's never looked better. The food is so awful that she's lost fifteen kilo. The experience has changed her completely. Taught her a lot about self-reliance, camaraderie, and an understanding of the difficulties of living in such a volatile spot. You should speak to her, Aggie."

"Tzillah, please. Aggie needs to make the right choice for herself. I'm sure Rachel's daughter has her reasons for choosing to serve far away from home and in a spot where there is no one around for miles and with no way to communicate with *her* mother. If Aggie were to lose even five kilo, she'd disappear. Besides she still has time to think about it. Right, dear?"

"Well, I—"

"This meal is the best ever, Eve." Dad leans back and sighs. "Aggie-doll, there's no reason why I can't pull in a few favors for my little sugarplum. Say the word and I'll see who I know and if they can't pull you into one of the better units. A good head like yours will be an asset to any unit."

"Yes, but—"

"Great, Aaron." Grandma sets her wineglass on the table, sloshing more over the side. "Just what the country needs: another government scandal. The papers would jump on it in a flash."

"Relax, Mother. She's a girl. It's not like pulling a son out from a combat unit. All I'm saying is that with a head like hers, she needs to be challenged in a place where her potential could be put to full use."

"Well, I was hoping to get into something on my own."

Grandma tosses her napkin on the table. "Now, that's the attitude I like to hear. Aggie can do whatever she wants—even if she is a *girl*, as you so eloquently put it. I want you to know that women like me helped make this country grow."

"Pure compost," says Mom.

"Eve!" says Dad.

Grandma chuckles. "If you can't take the heat," she says, holding up the hot pepper, "don't take the bite." She chomps down on the Moroccan hot pepper. Her face flames red, tears pour down her cheeks, and if she were a volcano, she'd be spewing lava. But she's not a volcano; she's my grandmother. She swallows. Takes a sip of wine and exhales.

"I had that one coming to me." She leans back in her chair. "But really, Eve. Life was tougher back then. We guarded the outposts. We healed the wounded. Old, young, frail, or female, we all had to fight. We didn't have the luxury of choosing, of—"

"Being born with a silver spoon in your mouth?" says Hila, holding up mom's flatware.

"Don't be impertinent," says Mom.

"I'm not trying to be. We could all set good examples. Imagine, Dad, if you turned vegetarian."

"The poultry farmers would tar and feather me." He laughs.

"So Aggie, what do you have in mind for your service?" I look at Grandma, who lights her third Marlboro of the evening. She clamps the cigarette between her thumb and fingers before taking a deep drag. A patriot. A Zionist. In her life, the second World War is more than a smudge on a history book. Grandma has tossed out the final and toughest question. I should have known it would come from her. She knows what it's like to hold a gun, fire it, and live with the consequences.

Where do I fit in? The food sits heavily in my stomach. I wish I had wings and could escape, but they have pinned me under their microscopes. Prove yourself, Aggie. Prove you deserve to be a part of us. Who are you, Aggie? Don't you know what you want? Don't you know how you want to serve the country?

"Well?" says Dad.

"Stop pressuring her," says Mom.

"Stop protecting her," says Hila. "What are you going to do, hold her hand through her whole army service? Iron her underwear?"

"That's enough, Hila." Grandma reaches over and places her nicotine-stained fingers over mine. "All we want is what's best for you. What's on your mind, Aggie dear?"

"Well, I . . ."

"Yes?" says Hila.

I take a trembling sip of wine and stare off at the

television, where Israel looks so small and squished by the giant landmasses that dwarf us on every border.

"Well, actually," I say, struggling to find my voice. "I was going to mention it earlier: the first field test for an elite combat unit for girls is next month. I passed the initial interview. They're letting me try out."

"Unbelievable," says Hila. "And you didn't tell me?"

"I was planning to." I ball up my napkin, holding it like a grenade without its pin. "If things go well, who knows?"

I swallow and wait. There is a moment of silence. I can't breathe.

Grandma taps the table with her lighter. Dad's eyebrows start dancing funny. Mom sucks in her lips and covers her mouth with her hand.

Hila breaks the silence.

It starts as a snort, followed by a juddering of her shoulders, and then a volcanic eruption of laughter. "Paratrooper Aggie," Hila spurts out between peals of laughter. "I love it."

Dad shakes his head. "Of all things, Aggie. What are you thinking?"

"Stop that, Aaron," says Mom. "You're hurting her feelings."

Mom's coming to my defense makes it all the more humiliating. The last swallow of food lodges in my chest. My eyes well up. It's hard to breathe. My shoulders crumple. I release the napkin. It's a dud. And I feel just as soiled and ready for the trash.

They're laughing. Laughing at the thought that I would even think of trying out for an elite combat unit for girls—and that an army as strong as ours would have use for someone as hopeless as me. I want to start crying. I want to get up, slam my chair against the table, tell them they're hurtful, horrible people, and then stomp out.

But they're just waiting for me to lose it, to have a temper tantrum so they can look at one another and say, "And she thinks she's elite soldier material."

So I just sit there, head bowed, counting the number of seconds it takes to fill my lungs and then exhale until I don't have a drop of air left inside of me.

I hear Grandma's lighter flick open and I look up. She lights another cigarette. Inhales and blows out a cloud of smoke. But no cloud is dense enough to hide the expression on her face. She winks at me and smirks.

"That's my girl," she says.

Chapter Three

Sunday morning and Jerusalem's central bus station is packed. The buses are crowded, and long lines of soldiers wait to board, going back to their base after an all-too-short weekend at home. I manage to struggle over and around the obstacle course of stuffed duffel bags and backpacks crowding the aisle and squeeze into the last remaining window seat.

Mom, Dad, and Hila stand outside the bus, waving.

"You'll do great!" shouts Hila. She blows me kisses.

Dad drapes his arm over Mom's shoulder, a satisfied smile on his face.

I wave back, a bit embarrassed that all these other soldiers are watching. But then I realize that the bus is oddly quiet. The soldiers have fallen asleep even before we've started moving.

I am too nervous to doze off and stare out the window. The soldier sitting beside me finally surrenders to the pull of gravity and his head slumps onto my shoulder. His rifle is propped between his legs. Every time we hit a bump, the barrel jabs me.

As we merge onto the highway, his cell phone raps out a version of the national anthem. It's so loud, the first time it rings I almost spring to attention and salute. He's out cold and doesn't hear it. We spend the rest of the ride together, me mouthing the words to his ring tone while he snores the chorus.

With his head bobbing on my shoulder, I lean against the partially open window, sucking in the air. Once out of the city, the sweet-sour smell of fresh cut hay wafts in from the farmlands around the mountains of Jerusalem. Trucks whiz by. Gradually the green turns to dried brush. Endless rocky hills remain unchanged but for the occasional village, connected only by the electric scarecrow towers strung with communication wires. The birds, perched in a lineup, wait for a sign before falling into formation and beginning their journey.

Eventually we pull off the highway and drive until all traces of green are replaced by the rocky red-brown earth of the Negev. Not the sand dunes of the Sinai in the south, here the earth crumbles, creating large craters and deep gashes. Though I've trekked over these jagged hills and inside the stony caves on several school trips, I still can't shake the feeling of enchantment every time I return.

The bus jerks to a stop. All the guys wake up as if on cue, wipe off their drool, grab their stuff, and start to disembark.

"We're here?" I ask the soldier beside me.

He yawns and for the first time turns to me. "Were you expecting a shopping mall?" He grins.

There's nothing else around for miles. It was a stupid question. The next stop anywhere could only be a tree if there was one. I reach for my backpack, stand up, and stretch. My foot needles me in pain.

"Excuse me," I say. Acting like I belong, I inch my way between the soldiers toward the front.

"Not you," the bus driver barks at me as I teeter at the top of the stairs. "The new girls stay put."

I plop back down. And don't move.

The soldier who had been using my shoulder as a pillow punches me lightly on the arm. "Take it easy," he says. "Good luck."

Having collected their gear, the soldiers head off

in the direction of the army camp, which is so well camouflaged I hadn't noticed it was there. Now sitting at the front of the bus, I can't tell how many other new girls are left besides me. I'm dying to look but am too nervous to twist around.

The bus drives on deeper into the desert along a road riddled with potholes. The band House of Dolls crackles through the static on the radio. A girl behind me joins in with the chorus, "And it seems like the dawn will never break," she sings.

Only ten minutes pass and again the driver lurches to a halt and opens his door. Nobody moves. I'm hoping he's just stopped to go out and relieve himself.

He turns around and with a wide grin says, "Now, girls. Out!"

No one questions him.

I grab my stuff and hurry down the steps, stealing a quick glance behind me. There are nine other girls. Jumping out of the bus, a gust of stifling hot air slams against me. I try and catch my breath. Get my bearings. If it weren't for the bus behind me, I'd swear we were alone on earth. How, in just two hours, can we have been transported from the bars, restaurants, and malls of the city into this vast stretch of nothingness, where there is only sun beating down, burnt hills, and rocky ridges?

As the other girls join me, the shuffling of their feet sends up dust clouds in my face. We don't speak. I've got that first-day-of-school feeling in the pit of my stomach. Squinting into the sun's glare, I search for a sign that there is something else here besides us.

The girl next to me grunts loudly and tugs at the underwear beneath her uniform. "Allo, hasn't anyone around here heard of sizes? Small, medium, plus for the full-sized woman?" She smoothes her hands down her thighs as if trying to shimmy herself into the tight parts.

I try not to laugh, but she looks as uncomfortable as I feel. "I don't buy that one-size-fits-all either," I say, hiking up my pants. We'd been given the clothes, equipment, and our identification tag numbers, and were told to get dressed before boarding the bus. I'd tried to get a smaller size uniform but had been brushed off. "You'll grow into them" had been the reply.

"If my pants were any higher, I could go undercover," complains another girl.

This time I allow myself to laugh out loud.

"Attention!"

We swing around. Three perfectly dressed soldiers have arrived from out of nowhere.

"I am your commander," says one of them, stepping forward. "You will call me 'Commander.' I will be in charge of you for these next few days." She eyes us critically. I shade my brow with my hand to get a better look at her. The sun is blinding. I try not to blink as she looks at me but am no match for either her or the sun's rays.

"Feet at a V," she barks, showing us the position. "Hands by your side. Chin up."

I straighten up. It's hotter than a roaring fire and it's only ten o'clock in the morning. My hand flirts with the canteen hanging on my belt. When I filled it earlier, I noticed how chewed up the rim was, which made me wonder how many slobbering mouths had used it before me. I thought nothing could make me touch it; now I'd give anything for a swig to quench my thirst.

I don't know how she does it, but the commander's uniform looks tailored to fit her body. She's not fat. Not thin either. She looks like she's made of stone slabs—except there isn't anything smooth about her. Thick, straight strands of reddish hair jut out from under her cap. Her steady gaze passes from one to the next as she looks up, nods, and checks off something on her clipboard propped in the crook of her arm.

"So you girls are here because you think that you are

tough enough to be in a combat unit? Tough enough to stick out a few days of training? Tough enough not to be bothered by dirt under your fingernails?"

The blond on my left glances at her red nails and discreetly closes her palms into fists.

"Well, I have news for you: when you're done, you'll need a team of archaeologists to dig the grime off of you."

The commander gestures with her hand toward the rocky terrain. "See this place? You won't find a coffee shop or pharmacy to buy baby wipes, but this is going to be your home for the next few days. Those of you who think you can't hack it, it's not too late to change your mind. Shmulik is waiting on the bus."

We all glance back at Shmulik. He pops his head out and waves.

The commander waits. My mouth feels dry. I suppress the cough tickling at the back of my throat.

"Nobody? I won't ask you again. But if you can't go on, just give us a sign and someone will drive you back to the base. Home-sweet-home is only a few hours away." She pauses to let her words sink in. "No one told you to try out for combat. You'll all have to do army service, but why choose the hard way?"

She stands perfectly still so that even the hot desert wind passes without ruffling a sleeve of her uniform.

There's a collective shuffle of boots. I'm standing next to the fat girl, who's already looking like she's got heat exhaustion just from standing in one spot. Her cheeks are flushed red and spotty. Go, I want to tell her. Why do this to yourself?

She doesn't budge. Neither do I, though I'm aware of the irony of this situation. This stand of defiance in response to our commander's taunt is an act of freedom of choice and is, if I make it through, the last free choice I'll make for the next two years.

"Fine. Stay if you insist. Your gear stays on the bus. Shmulik will drop it off in the evening." She waves to Shmulik and gives him the sign to push off.

We get a blast of exhaust, our last whiff of city life before the grind of the gears and the squeal of tires disappear and we're on our own. Not even a tree to protect us from the sun. No place to hide. There is an eerie emptiness. A quiet so heavy that it's as if we've entered into another zone not found on any map.

Our commander walks up to a redheaded girl and stands in front of her. I hear everyone draw in a deep breath. I wonder what she's done wrong.

The commander glances at her clipboard and back up at the girl.

"How's your Hebrew?" she asks.

It's a strange question and one after another we bend forward to get a look at the redhead, with the Number 30 tagged to her shoulder. She has tied her hair into a tight, cheek-ironed ponytail. The few strands that have escaped are pasted with sweat to the side of her face. From the corner of my eye, I dare a sideways glance. She is solidly built. No gust of wind will blow her over.

"I understand almost everything," the girl answers. Her American twang sends nervous giggles down the line. A new immigrant. I can usually spot the bewildered gaze and am surprised I hadn't noticed her earlier.

"And you're here on your own? Without your parents?"

She nods her head twice.

"Do you know the word in Hebrew for 'yes'?"

Again she nods twice but remembers to add, "*Ken*."

More giggles. It comes out sounding like "cane."

"*Ken*, what?"

"*Ken*, Commander?" she says.

Our commander nods, satisfied. "Okay. '*Ken*,

Commander' it'll be from now on." She turns and glares at us. "For all of you. Understood?"

"*Ken*, Commander," we reply.

The commander reads off her clipboard and her scowl deepens. She's not done with Number 30 just yet. "This says you came all the way from North Carolina to serve in the Israeli army."

"I was born here, near Haifa," she says, her voice dropping to a whisper. "My parents moved to the States when I was eight. I've got the right to do my service just like any of these other girls."

"Even though you could have gotten out of it."

"*Ken*, Commander," she says without a hint of a quiver in her voice.

"Let's hope that's a decision no one regrets."

I straighten up and feel the girls beside me do the same. The exercises haven't even started yet and already I feel I'm lagging behind.

Someone sneezes. I've left my tissues and toilet paper in my pack, which is now driving off with Shmulik to some unknown destination. The pit that had started to grow in my stomach in the morning feels crater size. I have never gone longer than twenty-four hours without my cell phone. I pat my empty pocket nervously.

"Now, drink up," the commander says.

Number 6, the girl with the blond cornrows, pulls out her canteen and takes a sip.

"All of it," the commander orders.

I start guzzling.

"When you're done, hold the canteen over your head. If more than one drop falls, fill it up from one of those jerricans," she says, motioning to a big black, plastic jug resting on a wagon, "and drink another full one."

I gulp the rest.

"You've got two minutes to relieve yourselves."

We look around. There's not even a bush in sight. Nobody moves.

"Good. Now we can start. See that hill?"

I suppose she means the one closest to us, though there are plenty others to choose from.

"*Ken*, Commander," we answer in unison.

"Well, you should have been there and back here forty seconds ago! Now. Run!"

We take off. I arrive third. My lungs are burning from the sudden burst of energy and the scorched air. But it wasn't that difficult. I think of Ben and how hard he made it sound. I wait for the others to finish. Catch my breath.

The commander looks at her watch. "That took sixty seconds. Again. Now. Run!"

We do it ten more times—each time worse than the time before. We slow down in the middle. We pause. We don't make it to the top of the hill. We don't wait for the last girl. My lungs are like sandpaper. My liver is bursting. My ego, deflated.

"Water break," she says. "Drink."

I gulp back as much as I can. But what do I need more of, air or water?

"Sip," says Number 16. "Or it'll slosh around inside your stomach when you run."

"Thanks." I take a sip and breathe, sip and breathe, until not a drop is left.

"My name is Amber," she says while we hold our empty canteens over our heads. "Like the orange-yellow stone."

"Hi," I say, and just as I'm about to ask her where she lives, the commander's voice bellows.

"See those sacks over there?" the commander points behind us. "And that pile of sand next to it? Fill the sacks with sand and seal them tight."

We nod.

"Full to the top. Is that understood?"

We nod again.

"Well? Move!"

And we're on the move. Ten girls. We rush toward the pile of sacks and grab them.

"Excuse me, Commander," says the fat girl confidently. "Did you forget to hand out shovels?"

"Number Twelve," the commander says, jotting down something on her clipboard. "What do you think?"

She shrugs and turns to us. "Use our hands?"

The commander nods. "Well, I was going to give you shovels, but since you asked, Number Twelve, I think hands are a better idea."

Silence.

Number 12 turns to us again, her cheeks even redder. "My friends call me Lily," she says apologetically.

No one answers her.

We kneel down and start scooping the sand and stuffing it into the bags. A fistful goes in as a handful spills out.

"This isn't working," I say, rolling onto my haunches.

The girls look at me, wondering if I'll be the first to quit.

"Let's work in pairs," I add quickly. "One holds the bag open; the other shovels sand in."

We get back to work. The word *why* threatens to tumble out of my mouth but I shove it back and tightly pack it away as tightly as the now-packed layers of sand.

I'm hoping Lily will have the nerve to say, "What now?"

But no one dares ask how much the bags will weigh when they're full or what we're supposed to do with them when we're done.

This is the army. We have been here barely an hour and have already learned the first two rules: Do as you're told. Don't ask questions.

Chapter Four

Besides, we find out soon enough.

"Haul them up. On your shoulders," the commander orders. "Remember that hill? Now get moving. Run!"

The sandbag slides and skids over my shoulder, hanging halfway down my back.

We tussle. The sandbag is as determined to bilk as much as I am determined to control it. The tall girl, with an Argentinean accent, rests her bag half on her head, half on her shoulder. I figure she's trying to do some Bedouin thing like the Arab women who carry baskets on their heads. After the first few minutes, she looks like, from her pinched-eyed squint, she's only succeeded in giving herself one major migraine.

"How many times?" asks Lily.

"Until I say stop." Our commander does not look

pleased. "And then you, Number Twelve, will do an extra one."

The girl from North Tel Aviv, with French-style polish on her fingernails, wrestles with her bag. She looks ready for a session of kickboxing.

"My baby cousin doesn't weigh much more," says Lily, panting, "and doesn't smell much better."

"Shh," says the girl behind me. "It'll just get them angry."

Involuntarily, I glance over at "them." The commander has two shadows following her, who are trailing us: two soldiers who don't look even a year older than me, holding clipboards and writing.

I speed up and reach the top of the hill in a pant. Only the second time of walking up the hill, down the other side, and back, and my right shoulder feels like it will never even out with the other one. I consider moving it to the other side, when the Tel Aviv girl comes to a sudden stop in front of me and tosses her sandbag on the ground.

"Stuff this!" she says. "I'm not wasting any more of my time hauling these stupid bags. I've got a brain. If the army needs someone to haul sand, I'll lend them my dad's truck or the worker who does our gardening."

She kicks the bag and without another look stalks off.

We stop and watch.

"Did I tell you girls to take a break?" The commander's voice slices the silence.

I step around the abandoned bag and shuffle on.

"Nine more sacks of sand on our backs, nine more sacks of sand. If one falls, we're one less brat and one less sack to haul," sings Lily.

"Enough!" the commander shouts.

"What?" asks Lily. "What's wrong with showing a little team spirit? I think we should be grateful to the Israel Defense Forces for training us in this very useful"—she stops to catch her breath, sees the commander looking at her, and speeds up—"task of hauling sacks."

I notice the scribes can't write fast enough.

"Stuff it, Lily," says Number 25.

"I've stuffed it as much as it's going to stuff. In fact, if we were to compare bags, I'd say yours was looking a bit on the anemic side. Don't suppose you feel like swapping, do you?"

I'd noticed it, too. Number 25 was short, stocky, and sweating buckets though her sandbag looked a lot less bulky than most of the others, mine included.

"Just teasing," says Lily.

We walk on.

My back hunches forward. The smell of sand is in my nose. My throat is raw. I have blisters on my ankles and each step scrapes off another layer of skin. I bite my lip. I try and focus on Lily's great green behind wobbling in front of me.

"Right. Left. Right. Left," I chant to myself. "If she can do it, I can do it. If she can do it, I can do it."

All we hear now is the crunching of our boots on the dry ground. We've got nothing in us left to spare. Even Lily has no words. My knee crumples beneath me. The second one follows. The ground feels so welcoming. I want to sit, lie down, take the weight off. Just a short rest, and I'll be able to go on. Right now, I've had enough.

The bag begins to slip from my shoulder. It feels so good to lighten the weight. I don't even care. This isn't for me. It's almost on the ground when I feel someone tug at the belt loop of my pants.

"Get up," Lily growls. "You've come this far, Twiggy. No cracking now!"

I straighten up and snarl right back at her. "Get off of me! And don't you ever call me Twiggy."

I dam back the tears and trudge behind her, wanting to use her big green backside for target practice. What does she care if I quit? Pulling me up. Pushing me forward. She's got nerve.

This is stupid. Carrying around weights of sand, what does that prove about me? Ben was right to say I'm more like a toy action figure than a combat soldier.

I can't anymore

I can't.

"I—"

"Lunch!" shouts the commander. "You've got forty-five minutes to eat and clear up."

In one orchestrated movement, nine sacks of sand plummet to the ground, followed by the sound of falling bodies.

Someone breaks into tears. She's snorting like a water hog. No one says anything because we're feeling about the same.

"I'm famished," says Lily. "Some of us need more fuel than others. Can you dehydrate from lack of food?"

I shrug.

The commander orders Number 6 to bring over a rucksack. Inside are cans of corn, cans of meat, cans of peas, and plastic containers of waxy-looking chocolate spread.

"I need meat," says the girl with the South American accent. "I could eat half a cow."

Number 6 slams down a can in front of her. "This is the closest thing you'll get to meat out here."

"Meat in a can?" Number 7 looks like she is about to faint. "Do you know how many preservatives there are in this? We eat only organically grown foods at home."

"Army rations," says the girl whose tears have dried to blackened streaks. "Get used to it."

"It looks like it's passed the 'best before' date," says Amber, squinting to read the fine print. "What year is it from?"

"Eat it or pass it here," says Lily.

"Do you want my peas instead?" I offer the vegetarian girl, holding out my can.

She shakes her head. "Thanks. But I need the protein to keep going. It's not like I'll get sick, right?"

No one answers.

I spread a layer of the canned meat on a slice of white bread, sprinkle corn kernels on top, and bite in.

Revolting, but I force it down. I know I need this to give me strength.

We're about done eating when suddenly the girl with the pigtails gasps.

"What's up?" asks Lily.

"Ohmigod," she whispers. "I think I just got my period."

"Oh geez," says Argentina. "Talk about bad timing. Does anybody have anything on them?"

"I brought," says North Carolina. She digs her hand into one of her pockets.

Pigtails groans again.

"Now what?" asks Lily.

"I need a bathroom. I need privacy." Her voice trembles. "What am I going to do?"

"We won't look," says one of the girls.

"I can't. It's too exposed."

I feel so bad for her. She'd carried her sand without even a grunt, not a single whine or curse.

"It's not fair," she cries.

She's right.

Lily points her sandwich at me. "Hey you," she says. "Grab your sandbag and put it here on mine."

I hesitate for only a second. "Good idea. We'll build her a wall."

"I'm not lifting sandbags on my break," says the girl with red fingernails.

"Yes, you are," says Lily.

And there is something in Lily's tone that makes everyone respond. In a few moments, Pigtails has a small wall to hide behind.

"I think we should all stretch out our muscles," says North Carolina. "I've taught aerobics at the Y. Seriously. I know about this stuff. We need to keep our lactic acids from building up and giving us cramps."

North Carolina takes a deep breath and stretches her arms up and over her head. Exhaling, she rolls down and hangs like a rag doll. "The trick is to inhale through your nose and exhale through your mouth." Her words come out garbled.

"You Americans are so conscientious," says Argentina. "Well, how about this." She pulls out a pack of cigarettes. "Inhale to the lungs." She lights up. "And exhale through the mouth."

"Get real," says North Carolina. "How are you going to run with lungs full of smoke?"

"I'm with the American on this one," says Lily. She plops herself on the ground, stretches, groans, yawns, and covers her face with her cap. "Am I stretching out all right?" she asks.

We all laugh.

North Carolina glances over at the commander. She lunges forward into some yoga contortion that Lily probably couldn't do on a normal day.

I know North Carolina is right and she's probably

scoring way too many extra points. I lie down next to Lily. "Hey, thanks for pulling me up back there. Sorry I was so snarky."

"Forget it."

I close my eyes and hear the rest of the girls filling in the space around me, worn, torn, and tired. All of us wondering: what in the world were we thinking when we volunteered for this? And are we going to make it through?

Chapter Five

"Five more minutes," the commander warns us.

"I'm picking up a very strong aura off of you," Number 7 says to me as she sits up.

I risk a discreet sniff of my underarms. The smell almost knocks me out.

"You're a Taurus, right?" she asks.

"Yes." My voice sounds tentative and suspicious.

"Taurus is ruled by Venus." She smiles. "That's the planet Noga, the one I'm named after. It represents love and desire." She gazes off into the distance. "Taurus are known to be stubborn." She nods her head. "If this"—she turns both palms upward and spreads them in front of her—"is what you want, you'll find the power inside you to overcome all obstacles. Taurus are survivors."

"And I'm sure right now I look like death."

Noga tilts her head to the sky. "Yes, but isn't it great not to have to care how we look? We're out here in the sun with nature and at one with the land." Noga's smooth light skin is dotted with dust freckles. She could be a poster girl for wholesome living if I hadn't just watched her polish off a can of meat.

"You sound like you're enjoying this."

"I could do without the sandbags." She pauses. "And I'd prefer being barefoot than wearing these clunky things." She struggles to lift her booted foot off the ground.

The commander whistles impatiently. "Lunch break is over. Number Six. Collect the garbage in that bag and put it by that pole."

"Why me?" she asks. "I brought the food. Someone else can collect the remains. It's not fair. I'm just as tired as they are. Why don't you make one of them do it?"

"I'll do it for Number Six," says Amber.

"My name's Sonya. And thanks."

"No you won't," says the commander. "You'll run up that hill and back, seeing as you've got all this extra energy."

"That's harsh," Lily mumbles.

We wait, wondering what Sonya will do. She looks at us, and the realization dawns that whatever she chooses will affect us.

Less than a second passes before Sonya picks up the garbage bag and begins to collect the trash.

I exhale.

"You five over there!" shouts the commander, pointing also at me.

Pigtails, North Carolina, Argentina, Amber, and I are given a stretcher. Doesn't look like a very sturdy thing: two long poles with a flimsy canvas in the middle. Still, I'm hoping that they'll volunteer me to lie on it, since I'm probably the lightest. And I could use the rest.

"Your sacks of sand. On the stretcher. Now!"

We heave our sacks on the stretcher. I can tell the other girls, like me, are feeling hopeful. Maybe we've finished this part of the exercise and it's time to pack in the sandbags and move on to something else. Anything would be better.

We slap the dust off our hands and grin at one another. The other girls stand beside their sandbags, looking disgruntled and jealous.

"You girls want to go into the field?"

"*Ken*, Commander."

"Then you've got to be able to carry each other out. When we're under enemy fire and you've got a man down, you'll do everything in your power to take him home. This is the army, but now"—she pauses and looks at each of us—"it's also your family. We never leave a soldier behind. You got that? Never. Now, lift it up!"

"Lift that?" says Argentina, pointing to the stretcher loaded with the sandbags. "But nobody weighs that much."

"Not even Lily," says Sonya.

"Hike the poles onto your shoulders. You four will hold it, and you," she says, pointing at Amber, "will run behind ready to switch off. The rest of you girls will carry the spare water canteens in those packs. Get moving. Keep it sturdy. Dropping an injured soldier could mean a life."

We each grab a side of the stretcher and heave it onto our shoulders. It seems to weigh more than everything I have ever carried in my whole life put together.

"Don't drop it," the commander warns. "It could be you up there one day."

I've cursed these sandbags and wished I could throw them into the sea. Now I'll do anything to keep the stretcher balanced on my shoulder. I don't want to be the one who drops it.

"My shoulder's killing me," says Carolina. "I can't do this much longer. Can someone switch me?"

"Who's on the stretcher, Private!" the commander shouts, running up to her.

No one answers.

We trudge on a bit faster, maybe thinking we can get away from her. I don't know what she wants. We don't have anyone up there, just our sandbags. Heavy, shoulder-crushing loads I'd like to toss over the next ridge.

"Who's on the stretcher, Private?" She waits another second. "The people who care about you the most, and who you worry about, are sometimes the heaviest ones to bear. The ones we'd like to rid ourselves of are the ones who give us strength. Who's on the stretcher, Private?"

"My ma," says North Carolina.

"Your mother?"

"Yes, Commander. My ma's been on my back for eighteen years."

No one speaks.

Her accent gets thicker. "Shouldn't you be studying, Hadas?" She pants and struggles for breath. "Shouldn't you be reading something more intellectual?" Her breath comes in short bursts. "Isn't that boy a bad influence on you? I've seen bathing suits with more material than that shirt you're wearing."

The commander motions to Amber to switch off with her.

"Tough stuff," mutters Argentina.

"Who's on your stretcher, Private!" the commander shouts at Argentina.

She staggers but catches herself. "My brother, Commander. My brother the Navy SEAL. My brother the genius. My brother the serious, successful one."

She switches off with Sonya.

We shuffle on.

I'm hoping she won't ask me. But she reads my mind.

"Who's on the stretcher, Private!" she hollers at me.

I don't know. My mind is blank. I can't think. Everything I've always wished for? Everything I've always wanted to be though I'm not even sure what it is. My head is reeling. The stretcher tears at my skin. My knees can no longer support me.

"Who's on the stretcher, Private! I can't hear you."

I trip on a stone, stumble, and the stretcher almost tumbles. Lily rushes forward and slides in, taking my spot.

"Good," she says to Lily. "That's how it should be done. Who's up there?"

The crunching of our boots, our labored breaths, and pathetic whimpers are the only sounds to break the silence.

"All one hundred sixty-five pounds of me, Commander—and that's before eating the calorie grenade we got for lunch."

Argentina laughs huskily. "We're lucky we've just got to carry the sandbags and not you."

The rest of us grit our teeth and keep moving. I can't help thinking that it takes a lot of guts to admit out loud that the thing that weighs you down the most is yourself.

We march on.

Twilight creeps in.

The commander whistles. We halt.

"Your duffel bags, tent, and sleeping equipment are waiting for you at the top of the next hill!" she shouts. "That's where you'll camp for the night."

"Up there?" whispers Amber.

"At the top of the hill?" says Pigtails.

We start the climb. My limbs don't feel like they belong to me anymore. Like used parts of some old machine that have been tossed together, they don't work in unison. My knees wobble. My boots slip on the gravelly dirt. My ankles quiver.

I'm walking behind Lily, putting my feet down in the spots where she put hers.

She starts to slip.

The top of the hill is in sight. Lily groans.

No! She's going to go down. I can't let that happen.

"Come on, Lily!" With a last burst of strength that comes from someplace inside, I bend my head, put both hands on her big round butt, and shove. I shove her as if she were a stalled car at the entrance to Jerusalem. Like all those cars that come so far and conk out so close to the top.

"Not after all you've done!" I shout at her. "We're almost at the top of our Jerusalem."

"Come on, Lily!" we shout in unison.

Chapter Six

We reach the top of the hill.
The sandbags fall to the ground with the stretcher.

"Good riddance," says Argentina. "If I never have to lift one of those again, I will be eternally grateful." She massages her neck.

"Amen," says Noga. She groans and sighs. "Look, a quarter moon. But no stars yet."

We glance up. The moon's glow begins to illuminate the distant hills. The heat, which had toasted us during the day, has burnt off. In this light the desert looks mysterious with the odd rock formations that curve in curious shapes.

"It's getting cold," says Amber. "What I wouldn't do for a hot shower."

Sonya groans. "A bubble bath," she says. "With

lots of scented bubbles to soak my feet."

The chill reminds me of the stuff I brought from home, the shower that I won't have but at least a clean T-shirt and a toothbrush.

"My teeth feel glued with grime," says Lily. Rinsing off her finger, she rubs it across her teeth.

I follow her lead, glancing over at the commander, who is talking with her scribes. We wait to find out what they have planned for us next.

Lily slaps me on the back. "You know, you did great today. How come you're so fit?"

"Jerusalem hills," I say, not sure if I've been complimented or insulted.

"There's got to be more. You're holding out on us."

I try and laugh it off but feel that the other girls are waiting to hear as well. I'm afraid they'll tease me, though there's no way to wheedle out of it now. "I dance."

Lily swivels her hips. "You don't look like the mambo type."

I roll my eyes. "Mambo? Me? No. Modern dance, some jazz, ballet."

"Now, that I can see. You're one of those Sugarpear Fairies."

Carolina giggles. "Sugarplum Fairy," she says. "I

danced in *The Nutcracker* when I was in grade six. One of the toy soldiers." She does a few steps.

"And from the way you're still going, I'd say they left the windup mechanism inside you," says Argentina through a cloud of cigarette smoke.

Carolina bats at the smoke.

"Okay, girls," says the commander. "It gets dark pretty fast around here. Number Eighteen will bring back the stretchers. The rest of you find your gear and start setting up camp. I've arranged a schedule of your shifts of guard duty throughout the night, which you will pass from one to the other. I expect you to be at your post on the hour assigned, and don't let me find one of you even thinking of drifting off while on duty. Understood?"

I straighten up the equipment and then head over to the pile of duffel bags.

"I actually brought *The Alchemist* with me," says Carolina. "As if I can keep my eyes open long enough to read."

"Or have the energy to lift the page."

The pile gets smaller. I'd borrowed Hila's navy blue backpack. It was the biggest one we had in the house. She used it when she went to camp. Navy blue is hard to see when there's so little light.

There are three bags left in the pile.

Lily takes one and trudges off. "It wasn't that heavy when I packed it this morning."

Pigtails takes the next.

Carolina grabs the last one. "Whew," she says. "For a second I thought it was lost."

There is none left.

But that's impossible. My bag has to be around somewhere.

Mine must have tumbled off to the side. Pigtails lends me her small keychain flashlight. The wind has picked up from the east. It's a sharp, thick wind carrying sandy grit. I raise my arm to shield my face.

"Did anyone see my sleeping bag?" I shout. "Or my backpack?"

There are a few mumbled replies; none of them sound encouraging. It's got to be here somewhere. I've got everything inside my bag. My toothbrush. A hairbrush. Hila gave me a pack of antiseptic wipes.

"Didn't anyone see where my stuff went?" My voice quivers on the edge of hysterics.

The tent is up. Noga struggles with the last pole, trying to straighten out the peculiar slant. Like moles, the girls have buried themselves inside. I'm alone. It's dark. There is a chill in the air that seeps in through my shirt and inside me. It must be dangerous to be out here on my own.

"Commander?" I tap on her tent.

"What?"

"My backpack is missing. I don't have a sleeping bag, a sweater, not even my hairbrush. What am I supposed to do?"

She pokes her head out of her tent. I see she has already rolled out her sleeping bag and unzipped it. Her two scribes are lying down.

"What do you want me to do about it?"

"I don't know." I can hear my voice breaking. "I put it on the bus with everyone else's stuff. How am I supposed to sleep?"

She looks at me with her cold, green glare.

I clench my teeth to keep from trembling.

"What do you want me to do about it?" She reaches for her radio. "I can call the base and tell them to come get you and take you home, if that's what you want."

She stares me straight in the eye. She doesn't even say it as a challenge. She doesn't care if I stay or go. Why should she? There are others who can take my place.

"Well?"

I don't know if that's what I want. I'm too tired to think straight. My head hurts. My mouth drops open but the words stay stuck inside.

"When you decide what it is you want, you come and tell me." She pops her head back in the tent. "I've had a long day."

She's had a long day? I find North Carolina outside the tent in a yoga pose. "Did you see my bag?"

"No."

I hesitate. "Do you think we could share a sleeping bag?"

Silence. "Sorry, but if I don't get a good night's sleep, I'll be hopeless tomorrow."

I get the same reply from the rest of the girls.

"Sugarpear," says Lily, "if I were to roll over accidentally, I might turn you into stewed fruit. Is that what you want?"

No, it's not what I want. I want to go home! I want to sleep in a warm bed with clean sheets. I want Mom to make me a cup of steaming hot chocolate. I want to hear Hila singing in the shower. I want Dad to tell me that everything will be okay. "Strength, Aggie-doll, is built from the inside out."

But I've had enough.

I head back to the commander's tent. The camping light she had on a few minutes ago is off. She's probably asleep. I stand outside working up the nerve to knock— but I'm too afraid to wake her. There's no one to ask and I don't even know which way it is to the army base.

I'm stuck!

I go back to the tent and slip inside. Lying on the rocky ground next to the open flap of the tent, I curl into a small ball. I'll wait for morning and then I'll have to leave. I feel something inside me beginning to snap.

Peeking up at the sky through the tent flap, I feel so small and overwhelmed by the vastness around me. I try not to whimper but can't stop myself. Something hits my foot. I scrunch up tighter. It lies near me. I kick it away. It doesn't move. Shining a light on it, I realize that someone has tossed out an old shirt.

I've become a dumping ground for dirty laundry.

Picking it up, I consider throwing it back, but the shirt is soft and smells clean, and rolled up, it works as a pillow, cushioning the rocky soil beneath my head.

A few moments later something itchy lands next to me. A wool sweater. It's not a blanket, but draped over my shoulders it keeps out the night chill.

For the next few minutes odds and ends fly my way.

Soon I've got a somewhat comfortable patch beneath me and am covered on top as well. The final thing lands with a jingle.

A stuffed bunny.

I can't believe someone brought a stuffed animal. Wrapping it in my arms, I snuggle down for the night.

Only I can't sleep.

It's the pressure.

I roll onto my side. I roll onto my stomach.

I try thinking about dry cleaners, dry crackers, dry toast, but nothing works. I have a sandbag inside me weighing down on the very spot where all the water that I drank but didn't sweat out is about to burst its dam.

I've got to go.

But it's dark.

I've got to go.

But it's too creepy to go alone. I'm bursting!

"Lily?"

Silence.

"Lily?" I say louder.

"What?"

"Don't you have to pee?"

I wait. A few minutes later her head pops out of her

sleeping bag. "Enough to flood the Jordan River."

Pigtails sits up. "Can I come, too?"

"Where are you going?" asks Argentina.

"To irrigate the desert," says Lily.

"Are we allowed?" asks Amber.

"What do you mean?"

We look at one another.

"We might not be allowed to leave here."

"We're not going out bar hopping," says Argentina.

"Maybe we should wake the commander and ask her."

"You wake her."

"Uh-uh. I'm not waking her."

"We could use a can and pass it around," Noga suggests.

"You want to take up a collection?"

"We'd share the can not the—"

"Disgusting." Lily wiggles out of her sleeping bag. "They can try and control my head, but there are parts of me that no one's going to ever control. Are you coming?" she says to me.

"I'm right behind you."

"Don't stand too close."

As we start walking, I hear movement behind me.

Soon eight of us are tiptoeing away from the camp,

down the hill, trying not to crunch too loudly in our boots. We scout the area for the most secure terrain.

"You three stand guard first," says Argentina.

"Why me?" says Sonya. "Why don't you stand guard first with Lily and the skinny girl?"

"My name is Aggie," I say. "And it was my idea to begin with."

"I'll guard first instead of Sonya," says Lily. "Just do it quickly, okay? I'm dying here."

Facing the ravine we unzip and crouch.

"All clear."

We switch. I keep an eye out. "Done?"

"Done."

"Done."

"Done."

Turning around, we tiptoe back up to camp, the mood a lot lighter. The others crawl into their sleeping bags. I slide between the shirts, sweaters, sheets, and pillowcases that were tossed my way.

"Are you okay Sugarpear?" asks Lily.

"Just me and the stars, but yeah, I'm okay."

"Hear oh Israel—"

Sonya groans. "Hey, how am I supposed to sleep with that racket?"

"I'm praying for us," says Noga.

"Pray for yourself. Preferably in silence."

"I was only going to ask Him to watch over us."

Sonya mutters something.

"Just because you don't believe," says Amber with a slur that can come only from a dental retainer, "doesn't mean you should be disrespectful."

"Thanks, Mom."

No one answers.

Argentina's raspy smoker's laugh is impossible not to recognize.

Then someone else joins in. Soon we're all laughing.

"We should get some sleep," says Pigtails. "Or we won't be laughing much tomorrow."

"Good night, Noga," says Sonya. She pauses. "I'm sorry I snapped at you."

"Don't worry about it," says Noga. "It's all in the stars."

Rolling onto my back, I peer out through the flap up at the stars. The sky seems so vast and far away. We must appear so little and insignificant from above. Who knows?

For now, I'm trying to think of all the right reasons to be here—but only the superficial ones come to mind.

If I make it through, Grandma will have something to boast about to her friends.

If I make it through, Mom—well, Mom will go berserk.

If I make it through, Dad will be impressed.

Hila will realize she's not the only one who fights for what she wants.

Ben and Ron will think it's sexy.

Shira will think it's dangerous and crazy, and that I'm out of my mind.

And Noah. If he were even to stop and think about it, he'd probably want to know how many constellations I saw.

"Big Dipper," I whisper, pointing at the sky.

"Are you sure?" he'll quiz me.

I'll explain to him how Grandma taught me to stargaze. After dinner on warm summer evenings she'd point out the Big Dipper, see if I could locate the northern star, and then she'd always have a word to add.

"Aggie, baby, remember that though we are small, nothing in this universe is insignificant. One drop of water can't create a flood. One grain of sand doesn't make a dam and one star can't form a constellation, but without the one, there would be none."

I whisper into the stuffed bunny's ear, adding, "And one soldier doesn't make an army."

Curling up with my knees to my chest, I try to conserve body heat. Sleep seems almost impossible . . . but just as I start to drift off, I am wrenched back with a shove on the shoulder and a cold burst of air as the sweater is yanked right off of me.

"Aggie," a harsh voice jars me awake. "Get up!"

Chapter Seven

"Hey!" I cry, tugging back the sweater.

"Get up already. I've been standing here for an hour trying to wake you."

The impatient whisper is unfamiliar. I try to ignore it by hunkering down deeper and falling back asleep, but the voice won't let me. My neck crimps. I knead the knot, tugging aside the steel fibers of the sweater draped over me. A gust of wind breezes down my shirt. Chilled. Hungry. Tired. Sore. Can't figure out which comes first.

"Go away," I grumble.

"I'm not going anywhere. Get moving before I turn you into a *mufletta*."

The visual comes back to me in full force. How could I not have recognized Lily's boom box?

I know it's her hulking over me, despite the dark circles rimming her eyes and the pinched scowl on her lips.

"Don't give me that look. It's your turn."

"My turn?"

"Your shift to guard. Come on. I'm exhausted."

And cranky. Her irritability is infectious. Sitting up, my motley beddings fall aside. "You don't have to hover," I snap at her. "Go on. You can see I'm ready." I stand up fully dressed, looking like I'm ready to march across the desert. We've all gone to sleep in our uniforms, including the boots on our feet. I wiggle my toes. I'm awake and now my toes decide to fall asleep.

Lily shuffles up dust and rubs her arms. "I'm not taking any chances that you won't bury yourself back under there. My shift ends once you're in place. *Hop* to it." She snickers, looking at the bunny still wrapped in my arms.

Tossing the stuffed animal back on the lump of bedding, I scoop up the ends of my hair and rein them in with my now-blackened scrunchie.

"Noga's after you, at two o'clock," says Lily. She points to the guard post, which isn't much of a post. All that marks the area is a flat rock on a mountain rise. Inside, a burning burlap sack sends up fumes.

"Now I could use some sun," I say. My army-supplied jacket is together with the rest of my gear: lost. The scorching desert sun has gathered up all its heat and left a dark chill behind.

Lily shrugs and hands me the list. It's already two minutes past her hour. She yawns. Her whole body judders, all the way to her tonsils.

"Whatever you do, don't fall asleep, or you'll get tossed out of here—fast."

I look around. Night has turned the desert upside down. Above, the sky stretches endlessly, and now it is too dark to see even a meter beyond where I am standing.

"Is it dangerous?"

Lily shrugs. "Don't know. It's a bit creepy being alone. I tried not to think about it too much." She starts to walk back to her tent. Stops. Groans and turns back.

"What now?" I ask.

"Here," she says, shirking off her jacket. "You'll freeze without this. Just give it back to me in the morning. I'm not getting fined because you can't hold on to your things."

"It's not my fault they're missing."

But she's already gone, hurrying off to the tent.

Grateful, I swaddle inside the oversized coat, thinking how Lily is like one of those sour candies with a sweet, chewy center. I lick my lips and dig into her pockets. Jackpot! Contraband jelly beans.

I pop a few, hoping that Lily either won't notice them missing or won't mind. She had to have known she'd left them behind. The loan of the jacket came with the pockets.

Quiet. I've never heard such quiet. No sirens. No neighbors. Eerie, like Lily said, but also peaceful.

A jackal howls.

I toss a few more jelly beans in my mouth, but the sound of my chewing is too loud. Rather than feeling frightened, for the first time since arriving, a sensation of calmness settles over me. All the tension of the day seems to drain into the land. It feels almost biblical. I imagine how Abraham must have felt out here.

Holding a palm full of jelly beans, I pick out the black licorice ones and eat them first.

A wind breezes by. I tuck strands of loose hair behind my ear. The ends prickle me. My skin bristles. Exhaustion is turning my body into an inverted cactus.

According to my watch, only ten minutes have

passed. I check to make sure it's working.

In the distance, a snore. Have to tell Hila about this. She'll flip. Alone in the desert after a grueling day, no sleeping bag, no sleep. I hardly believe I'm still standing!

The jackal howls again. No point in looking for it. The darkness is like an opaque veil allowing only bits of starlight to shine through.

Stretch. On my toes. Heels. Yawn. An unfamiliar tune pops into my head. The American girl was humming it earlier. "An indie group," she'd said.

I do a few pliés and relevés. Roll my shoulders. Point my toes. Flex. Five minutes pass. All's quiet. A few more snores and some murmurs from the tents. What now? Wonder what Noah thinks about when he's standing guard. Haven't told Shira about Noah, or even about what happened with Ben. Will she be annoyed, jealous?

Twenty minutes left. First forty already gone.

Had Ben made a move back in junior high, it would be different. But now there's Noah. Noah . . . Just thinking of him is like having a sweet swig of hot cappuccino.

Ten minutes to go.

Need some sleep before tomorrow.

Tomorrow. Will I make it through another day of sandbags and stretchers? Someone is bound to break soon. Which one of us will drop? Lily? No, she's carrying a lot of extra weight, but she's so determined, nothing will stop her.

Sixty seconds left. Thirty-nine. Twenty-four. Twenty-three. Twelve. Eleven. Yes! Done! Did it!

Almost skip back to the campsite. Just want to put my head down, close my eyes. Hug my bunny. Sleep the last few hours before they wake us.

"Noga." I jiggle her shoulder.

No answer.

There's a sour smell about her.

"Noga. Your turn. Get up."

She groans. "Can't."

"Come on, Noga. I need to get some sleep."

I feel that same pinched expression that Lily wore when she bent over me.

"Can't move," she says. "My stomach."

"Get up and you'll get over it."

"But my stomach hurts." She moans. "It must have been that non-vegetarian food I ate."

"You mean the meat."

She groans again. "Meat," she cries. "I think I'm going

to be sick. Canned meat. I think I've got food poisoning. Get someone else to take my spot."

"Are you out of your mind?"

She groans and starts to rock.

"You're no sicker than the rest of us. You're tired. Now, get moving."

"Aggie, please. I can't."

What am I going to do? The shift after Noga's is Sonya's. I know she won't start before three o'clock. And even if she does, we'll still be missing someone for the last hour. Noga pulls the sleeping bag over her head.

Glancing longingly at my makeshift bed, I trudge back to my post.

Just do it, I tell myself. Noga would have done the same for me, were the situation reversed. After tomorrow I'll sleep for a solid week.

Stretch. Jiggle my limbs loose. Sing a few bars of the Shlomo Artzi song Shira loves, about waiting for the Messiah, who's taking his time in coming. I stop in the middle as a sound disrupts the silence.

Footsteps.

They crunch. Boots moving in my direction. My breath catches in my throat. Every nerve tenses. I wait as a figure takes shape through the darkness.

"Private."

"Ken, HaMifaked!" I answer, snapping to attention.

"Identify yourself."

"Abigail. I mean, Jacobs. Jacobs." I pause. "Abigail."

"Number."

"Eighteen."

She looks at the list in her hand and scowls. "This isn't your shift."

I shake my head. "My shift was last hour."

"Where's Number Seven?"

"Not feeling well, *HaMifaked*. Stomach cramps."

The commander looks at me. "Who told you to replace her?"

Her tone is heavy with accusation. I've taken something upon myself. I've made a decision without consulting her.

"No one," I mumble.

She looks at me. "You weren't tired enough and so you decided to do an extra shift?"

I shake my head. "No. It's—it's," I stutter.

"What is it?"

My throat, like the desert, feels dry. "I thought—I thought it would be worse to leave the post unguarded."

She looks at me. Her shoulders squared. Her lips pulled

tight. And her eyes, tiny slits of greenish gray beneath her sharp brows, seem to ask a different question.

Why am I doing this? Am I trying to prove something? Who will know? Sonya will know when I wake her. So will Noga, tomorrow. Will they thank me? Or resent me? Confusion jostles with anxiety. This is the army. I'm not allowed to make decisions. What if she thinks I'm trying too hard. What if— But what should I have done instead?

The commander pulls out a cigarette, lights it, and squints at me through the smoke as she slowly exhales. "We aren't carrying the stretchers anymore, Number Eighteen."

I lower my eyes. She has seen through me.

She flicks away the cigarette. It hits the ground, glowing. She pulls out a Thermos from her backpack and carefully unscrews the top. The steam rises in little smoky wisps. I watch the trails of steam, wishing I could catch them. There is a hollow pit in my stomach made worse by exhaustion and hunger. She pours herself a cup of hot coffee.

I've made a mistake. Wanting this so badly, I've gone too far. And in trying to prove myself, I've messed up. I blink back the tears that would only mock me.

The commander takes a sip. "Ahh," she sighs. "That hits the spot. It's with milk and sugar," she says. "Just the way I like it."

"*Ken*, Commander." My voice quivers.

And then a smile cracks the corners of her lips, and she hands the cup to me. "Drink up, Private. You've earned it."

Chapter Eight

Night merges into morning. The sun grows stronger as noon approaches. Not even a Bedouin woman or a stray donkey passes by to break the monotony. I have barely caught my breath from the last exercise before the next one begins.

"Line up!" the commander hollers. "Now we'll test your survival skills."

"I thought they did that yesterday with what they served for lunch," Argentina mutters.

"You will be given a map of your route. But not a tourist's street map, a topographical map. See that hill we climbed yesterday? This is what it looks like here." She spreads the map on the ground.

She points to other spots, giving us a crash course in geography.

"I've grouped you in pairs. You will be dropped off five kilometers from the army base you passed on the way here."

"We're going back?" asks Amber.

The commander gives her a look. "That depends on you."

I can tell by her tone that it won't be as easy as it sounds.

"You will learn the route. Memorize it. And trusting your memory, get back to base camp as soon as possible. You will be given a compass and water as well. But you may not look at the map. If you open the map, we will know. Use it only in dire circumstances."

She pauses and the corners of her lips turn up. "The first ones back will be the first to shower in hot water. The water gets progressively cooler as the tank empties."

I scratch at a black glob of dirt on my arm. Stubborn. I scratch harder. It's a tick. I wrench it off and flick it away.

The commander studies her clipboard. I'm hoping to be paired up with Pigtails. We worked well together on the last exercise. Besides, she has a flashlight. Someone with a flashlight surely knows how to navigate.

"Number Eighteen."

I step forward.

"Number Twelve."

Lily steps out from the end of the line.

The commander looks at us both and hands me a map and Lily the highlighter. "You will begin here." I follow her finger as it snakes its way along the map.

"Lily—the highlighter." I snatch it from her and start tracing the route.

"Any questions?"

I make room for Lily to go over it as well. She is picking at her thumb. "I think I've got a hangnail."

"I'll give you ten minutes to memorize it," says the commander.

I focus on the route. "Lily, are you looking?"

"I think it might be infected."

I want to tell her she'll have more to deal with than just a hangnail if she doesn't look at the map. Since I'm short, about two of my steps are a meter. According to the map, we go a hundred meters west—about two hundred of my steps—turn one kilometer north, turn west again for fifty meters, and then go straight the last bit—straight into the showers.

"Fold it up and put it away."

I take one last look and then fold it. The commander

seals the map with tape and tucks it into my breast pocket.

"Let's hope it stays there."

"*Ken*, Commander."

The scab on Lily's thumb is bleeding. She raises her thumb to her mouth, thinks better of it, and wipes her hand down her pants.

"Fill up your water canteens. Drink one full one now and then refill it for later."

We head to the water tank while the other girls get their routes. Lily strolls over like we're going for a hike in the country with a stop first at the snack bar. When her canteen is full, she gives it a shake to show that she's following the rules and knows to make sure no water is sloshing around, and then hops on the jeep.

The jeep drops us off somewhere between where we were and where we're supposed to get to. The driver spins the tires, spewing up dust and sand in case we weren't covered enough to begin with. The sun beats on us from above.

"South," I say. Sun's almost overhead. I double check the compass. "We start here."

"You think so?"

"Yes, I do, because I was looking at the map."

Lily takes off her army shirt. She's wearing only a tank top underneath. Rolls of flesh spill out from every side. "It's so hot." She fans herself.

"Two hundred meters this way." I start walking. "One, two, three . . ."

Lily follows. "That driver was yummy."

"One hundred and twelve—"

"Did you see the way he smiled at me?"

"One hundred and sixty-three, sixty-four—"

"I should have asked him his name again."

"One hundred and seventy—Lily, will you shut up? You're confusing me."

We reach two hundred.

"Now we go one kilometer north."

"I think he said his name was Ariel or maybe Daniel? Did you get his name?"

"Lily, I'm trying to concentrate!"

I'm not sure I've counted right. Maybe my steps were bigger than usual because Lily kept scraping at my heels. But no, there was a hill on the map. Yes. This must be right. We walk in silence for the next few meters. I focus, trying to feel how far a kilometer is. Now we go . . .

"East or west?"

"East or west what?" asks Lily.

"I'm blanking out. Do we turn east now or west? I don't remember. I know it's fifty meters, but I don't remember which way." I spin around and can't get centered. "Which way?"

"Calm down. You're going berserk."

"Calm down? You weren't even looking at the map! You were picking at that disgusting scab on your thumb. Now what? Which way?"

I try and catch my breath, but it's going faster than me. I have no clue where we are. My instincts are clogged. "I've messed up—totally! Which way do we go?"

"Relax. I've got everything under control. This way," she says.

"How do you know?"

She stares me down. "Instinct."

"Instinct?"

"What's wrong? You don't think I have instinct? I have instinct. Didn't I tell you the way that yummy driver was ogling me? It's called having a sixth sense. I am a very sensual person."

I force back the desire to strangle her and unscrew the cap on my canteen instead. Lily does the same.

"L'Chaim," she says, clinking our plastic.

"If we live to get out of here—"

Lily laughs. "You're used to depending on that brain of yours, aren't you? The way you figured out that crossing-the-river exercise—very impressive."

"Thanks." I take another swig of water. Before heading out on that survival test, we'd been given a barrel, a rubber tire, a log, and told to imagine a river beneath us. I figured out how to get us all across. "Just using basic logic."

"No. You've got a brain."

"Lot of good it's doing me now."

"That's why they put us together. You've got it up there." She points to my head. "And I've got it here." She jabs at a spot on her sweaty cleavage. "Instinct," she says.

"Well—I'd just like to have a little more proof than your instinct, which might have us wandering around in the desert for the next forty years."

"Proof? Proof is that I know the base is that way and you are not sure."

I look "that way." It doesn't look any different than any other way. There are rolling hills, rocks, and bramble bushes. I rub my eyes. Lily is convinced. She starts to walk.

"Follow me," she says.

I hurry up to reach her. I think I'd rather be lost in the desert with someone than lost on my own.

"Can you just stop for a second? Maybe we should check the map?"

"We're not supposed to, and I don't know how to read those things. I follow my gut."

I swear she's almost trotting. I jog up beside her. "How is it that you are so sure you know where you're going?"

"Trust me."

"Why? Give me one good reason"—my voice wavers on hysteria—"why I should trust you?"

She sticks her sweaty face in mine. "Wake up. When do you ever think you'll be stranded in the desert with no map and only a compass to guide you?"

I plant myself in front of her and don't step back. Her body is oozing heat and sweat and between us there is an electric charge so hot it could burn a hole in the ozone. "Now!" I yell. "Now we are stranded in the desert with only a compass. If your instincts are guiding us in the wrong direction, we won't be showering for the next week, never mind the next few hours."

"My instincts are impeccable. What's lacking is your trust. Can't you trust me enough to get you back?"

I take a deep breath. I don't have much choice. If I

look at the map, we'll be disqualified. If I go with Lily, we might arrive, and then if we don't, we'll be disqualified anyway.

"Okay. Since I don't know which way to go and you say you do. Lead on."

She turns her back to me. I jump around in front of her in time to see her slip something into her pocket.

"What was that?"

"Nothing."

"It's not nothing. I saw you holding something."

She sighs. "Okay, Aggie. You caught me. I surrender."

She pulls out a small palm-sized instrument.

"GPS!"

"Shh!" She puts up a hand to hush me even though there's no one in sight. "Sound travels in the desert. If the other girls hear you, we'll have the whole bunch of them here."

I stamp my foot. "Lily, you'll get us disqualified. You'll get us thrown out. How could you do this without asking me? You know we're supposed to be trying to figure this out on our own. I trusted you." I take a deep breath, fighting for control. "We've come so close to finishing and now you pull this kind of stunt. What were you thinking?"

Lily stands in front of me and crosses her arm over her chest. "I was thinking," she says, "that I need this more than you do. If you fail, you'll use that brain of yours and your connections to get some high and mighty position. You don't need to pass these field tests. This is just a game for you."

"That's not true." My voice wavers.

Lily has her hands on her hips and cocks her head at me. "You know it's true. Here's your proof: you can't even look at me when you defend yourself. And see, if I don't pass this test, what's waiting for me? I'll get stuck behind a desk where I'll be making coffee for some general and maybe getting my behind pinched by whoever's walking by at the moment."

She wipes the sweat from the back of her neck. "So, are you coming with me or are you going to stand there on your high horse preaching about honesty, integrity, and equality for all?"

"But it's cheating. It's not right."

Lily snorts. "Where did they find you? Beam you from Planet Virgo? If you've never done anything underhanded, then you haven't been living in this life. Life doesn't follow strict rules. It makes them up as you go along. So to keep one step ahead, you just have to be sharper and quicker and not let anyone grab your behind because you're already five steps out of their reach."

"We could have figured it out on our own."

"Give it a rest. We haven't been drafted yet and we certainly won't die out here looking for our way back to base to take a shower. It's not real life. And you can trust me. I'll get us back to the base in no time."

"It feels cheap," I say.

Lily laughs. "What's wrong with getting the same boots for a good bargain at the market that would cost you a whole lot more in a fancy store?"

For all my supposed braininess, she's got me stumped on that one.

Chapter Nine

Being angry with Lily is just too hard. About ten meters after our argument she breaks into the chorus of the song I hate the most.

"I'm walking through the desert with no horse and no name." She's doing the chicken walk and sticking her neck out on every beat.

Suddenly I spot, jutting out of the rocks, two poles waving blue-and-white flags with the Star of David on them.

"Base!" I shout. In the distance a few tents and barracks stand out against the endlessly blue and unchanging desert sky. Like a fata morgana, out of nothingness the base begins to take shape. A command car is parked at the entrance, where strains of a familiar tune from the radio break the silence. A bus pulls up to the entrance and passes through. The high barbed-wire fence looping around the perimeter with points like cactus spikes should be threatening, but right now I couldn't imagine a more enticing sight.

"You mean we really made it?" says Lily.

"We did. We made it!"

"Hallelujah! This thing really works."

Lily and I throw our sticky arms around each other and start dancing. "We made it! We made it!"

Arm-in-arm, romping and shouting, we dance our way to the entrance of the base, where two Rambo-style soldiers are standing guard. I tug off my army shirt and twirl it in the air. We must look ridiculous, but I don't care. My tank top clings to my chest, glued on by hours of sweat and filth.

"You guys look good enough to hug," says Lily.

"Yeah," says Rambo Number One, "but you girls don't. Not like that anyway. Got soap?" he says.

"Soap!" Lily sings. "Soap and shampoo! What would I do without soap and shampoo? Feeling so good. Can't wait to be clean. Rid my bod of these ugly greens—"

"Lily, enough! They get the point." Our sweaty, dirt-stained bodies coupled with shouts of joy are all they need for identification, and they let us onto the base.

"Follow the lime-powdered stones on your right to the third set of barracks," says the amused soldier. "Your commander will meet you there."

Like Dorothy on her way to Oz, we skip down the path that hugs the perimeter of the base. It's after lunchtime, but I swear I smell schnitzel frying. A signpost points to the dining room behind us. I'm hungry—but first I need to shower.

"Soap and shampoo," we sing. "What would we do without soap and shampoo . . ."

We reach the third set of barracks, dash past the flagpole, and scout for the showers.

"Over here!" shouts Lily. "And they're empty. Yes!"

I'm yanking at my rope belt as I run when a familiar voice stops me cold.

"So you've made it back."

"*Ken*, Commander." We snap to attention. Feet at a V. Arms by our sides.

"And where are you going now?"

"To shower?" I remind her. "You said we could shower when we got back." Something behind my knee is itching to be scratched. I imagine my whole body crawling with ticks and ants and desert parasites. I need to shower. I need to scrub my body clean. The hunger and exhaustion I felt before seem inconsequential compared to my burning need to wash my body clean.

The commander doesn't move. She looks us up and down. She's showered. She's changed her uniform and even blow-dried her hair. She looks at my tank top. I slip on my army shirt.

"What about the others?" she asks.

"The others?" asks Lily. She's pulled her shirt back on, too, but hasn't buttoned it up.

"Don't you think it only fair that you wait for the other girls to arrive so that you can all shower together?"

We both know the right answer. She's not commanding us; she's not forcing us. But from the tone of her voice we know that there is only one right answer, the one she wants to hear.

"Of course," says Lily.

"Good." The commander points to a tent beyond the barracks. "We'll gather there for a short recap and then you can *all* go off to the showers." She starts to walk away and stops. "By the way, Eighteen, you'll find your bag with the rest of the girls' stuff."

"Thank you," I say, though it's hard to sound sincere. Lily and I trudge over to the tent.

"We were so close," she mutters. "She promised that the first ones back could shower first."

"Just a little bit longer," I tell her.

The tent is a huge canvas tarp propped on poles and open on all sides. A few chairs, a ratty sofa, stuffed pillows, and some tables are scattered underneath it.

"Finally," says Noga as we walk in.

She's got big ugly scratches on her face and down her arm.

"What happened to you?" asked Lily.

"Why?"

She hasn't got a clue how bad she looks. Mirror deprivation. I'm afraid to see the effect it's had on me.

"Nothing," says Lily.

Pigtails answers for her. "She got her foot stuck and tripped into a thornbush. What took you guys so long?"

"Our Lamborghini stalled at the last water hole," says Lily. "What do you mean, what took us so long? At least we're here. We can't shower until the rest of them show up anyway."

The four of us sit and wait. Rolling up my pant leg, I see that I haven't been imagining it: my leg is covered in strange, red blotchy dots. I scratch.

Gradually the tent fills. Argentina and Amber, flushed and looking like they're on the brink of dehydration, arrive last.

"Good, you all made it back," says the commander. She nods at Pigtails and Noga. "The two of you did a commendable job. You were back first. Did you need the map?"

Pigtails shakes her head. "No."

"Who led?"

Pigtails rubs her hands on her knees. "Well, Noga collected a lot of beautiful rocks for her collection of moon-glazed stones."

Lily laughs. "I bet."

"That's enough. This exercise is as much about getting from one place to another as it is about working together." She turns to me and Lily. "You two also managed to get back here quite quickly."

I nod. I can't look at Lily.

"Do you have anything you'd like to share with us?"

I shake my head.

Lily doesn't say anything either, so I gather she's giving her blank stare.

"Did you have to look at the map?"

I shake my head.

"Did you want to?"

I nod my head.

"And how did you get along?"

"We argued some," says Lily. "But then Aggie decided to, uh, see things my way, and so we worked things out."

The scribes write furiously on their clipboards.

My eye is twitching. I pretend I've got some dirt in it and rub until it stops.

The commander turns to Amber. "If your partner wanted to look at the map and you didn't and in the end she did and that's what got you back here, would you admit to having used it?"

She swallows. "Would it mean failing this test?"

The commander doesn't answer. She's got the look of a sniper. No detail goes unnoticed. "Where are your loyalties, girls? To the army? To each other?"

Amber chews on her sun-chapped lip. She's struggling.

The pit in my stomach is getting bigger. Lily sits beside me, but I think she's stopped breathing. She's not waiting to hear what Amber has to say; she's waiting to see what I'll do.

If I confess that we've cheated, we'll both be disqualified.

"It's complicated," says Amber. "It's like a bit of both."

The commander waits. "That's not a good enough answer."

Loyalty. I swallow. I'm not thinking about the big reasons. I'm thinking of Lily, who wants more than anything to be accepted into this combat unit. Lily is a leader. She has instincts. I realize that I'd want her on my team. And if the sacks of sand, the dirt, the ticks, the scabs, and an infected hangnail didn't break her, who am I to pull her down?

"It is both," I say, looking at Lily. "If we aren't loyal, then how can we learn trust—and isn't trust essential in knowing that you can rely on each other when it really matters?"

Noga nods vigorously. "Exactly."

"Up to a point," adds Amber.

"There's got to be a point," says Pigtails. "I'm just not sure I can define it for you yet."

I agree, but like Pigtails, I'm not sure where we're supposed to draw the line. I'm not sure it's something we could all agree upon.

The commander has a facial expression that I'm finding hard to read. Her lips have curled up at the corners and she seems—yes, she appears to be smiling. My heart feels like it's bursting.

"Congratulations. I think you girls deserve to get cleaned up before you go home and celebrate."

"You mean, we made it?" asks Pigtails.

"I mean that you've succeeded in getting through this part of the exercise."

"Can we go shower now?" asks Carolina.

"That's an order." She makes a face. "It's getting hard to be around you girls."

We rush out of the tent and cut back toward the barracks.

"Did you see the way she smiled at us?" I say. "I thought I was going to die."

"That'll be you one of these days," says Lily, stripping off her army shirt as she runs.

I'm right behind her when I hear a guy's voice calling me.

"Aggie?"

I spin around. I'd recognize his voice anywhere, deep and kind of husky, the kind of voice that'll give you goose bumps even in the heat of the desert.

"Aggie!"

I'm wearing only my stinky undershirt splotched with

shades of black and gray. My hair is layered with last night's brush pillow, and the only reason I know I must smell pretty bad is because all the other girls around me smell awful. And there is Noah! He's waving his arm and coming over to greet me, like this is a bar in Tel Aviv and he's out with a bunch of guys I've never seen before.

"Help," I squeak, turning to Lily. "Hide me." I'm standing by the flagpole in the open area outside the barracks. There isn't a tree, brush, or manhole anywhere.

She shakes her head and laughs. "Who's the hunk?"

Before I can explain, Noah is standing in front of me. He has dark camouflage paint under his eyes that makes him look raccoonlike. Behind me the girls have stopped to stare.

"Noah? What are you doing here?"

"We just got back from a week of survival exercises, and we saw these girls dancing outside the base. I couldn't believe it, and then I realized, wait a minute: I know that girl—and it was you!" He gives me a full-dimple smile.

I cover my face. "How embarrassing."

He laughs. "It was too good to be true. But what are you doing here?" He pushes up the sleeves on his uniform. I notice burn marks on the inside of his arm: small ovals the size of bullet shells.

"We just got back from an overnight field test."

He raises his eyebrows, a puzzled smile on his lips.

"I think I've just passed the first test to get into a combat unit." It feels so strange and unbelievably terrifying to actually say it out loud.

"Combat?"

"You sound surprised."

"Not for a second," he says, his dimples playing a game of hide-and-seek. He rubs his chin, where a scruff of beard has grown since the last time I saw him. "It takes a certain type."

The girls have fallen silent. I can feel them grouping behind me. "And you don't think I'm that type?"

"No, not at all," he says, quickly. "That's not what I meant."

"What did you mean?" I'm about to step closer and quiz him when I remember that I'm preshower. My face turns bright red—not that he would notice under the layer of grime.

"Aggie," says Lily, "are you planning on showering in *hot* water?" She grabs my arm and pulls me back.

Noah fiddles with the gun strap across his chest like I've seen him do with his guitar strap. "They're giving us a night off so I'm going home now." He clears his throat.

"Maybe we can continue talking about this later, at my house."

"Hey, Noah," says one of the other raccoon-faced soldiers. "Why don't you introduce us to her friends?"

"After a shower, buddy," says Argentina.

"She's got a point. Later, Number Eighteen," says Noah, giving my tag a playful flick. And he walks off, leaving me wondering yet again if he's teasing me and why these meetings with him make me feel so confused. Then as I run my fingers through my hair, I remember how I must look.

"Ohmigod. I can't believe he came within a kilometer of me. I'm disgusting."

Lily laughs. "And did you get a look at him?"

"Did I ever; didn't you?"

Lily groans. "You spent one night in the field without a shower. He's been there a week. You do the math."

She drags me to the bathroom, where all nine of us strip naked and soap up.

"Heaven," I moan as the dirt washes away in rivers by my feet.

Of course the hot water finishes faster than it takes us to lather up, but who cares?

As I'm tying up the laces on my running shoes, a

shadow falls over me. Looking up, I see Lily wearing a tight burgundy tank top, low-riding black jeans, and dangerous heels. She smells like an overgrown botanical garden. Three gold bangles loop from her right ear and she has a single stud in the left. Her eyelashes look like they've sprouted another foot in the last five minutes.

"Wow! You look—you look . . ." Words fail me.

Lily laughs. "Hang around me and you'll learn everything you've got to know about accessorizing. First you need to get yourself one of them padded push-ups." She punches me in the arm. "Just kidding. Anyway. Congratulations, Sugarpear," she says. "We did it."

"There were a few moments there when I wasn't so sure we would."

"Loyalty. Trust. Friendship," she says, and smiles at me, a full-toothed Lily grin. "Believing in yourself as much as you do the other guy. That's what's important. Through fire and water." She hoots. "Yesterday when I saw you get off the bus I thought, 'That one won't make it past lunch.' But you did. You're a real fighter." She pauses. "And thanks to you, I passed, too."

I shrug, and hope she can't read my mind, especially the thoughts I'd had about her earlier. But now I feel the kind of bond with her that took Shira and me years to build.

"The commander said I've got to keep my weight up, though. If I drop under fifty kilo, they may reconsider."

"Now that's one problem I've never had to deal with! Take down my cell phone number. A couple of my mom's meals and you'll have all the extra weight you'll need. I am living proof."

We exchange numbers. Grabbing our bags, we head for the bus.

"I can't wait to get home," says Pigtails. "I think I miss my chickens more than anything."

"A kibbutz girl," says Argentina. "No wonder the dirt didn't faze her. She lives for the smell of cow."

"Hey—"

"She's teasing, Pigtails," says Noga. "You were an inspiration."

Pigtails beams. "You're all welcome to come and visit me anytime."

We hear the grinding gears of the bus before we see it round the hill.

"My boyfriend sent me one hundred twenty-two text messages." Noga's phone beeps in another one. "He's already waiting for me at the bus depot."

"How about you, Sugarpear?"

"Another hot shower. Dinner and then—" And then Noah, I think but am too shy to say. "What about you?" I ask her. "What are you doing later?"

"I'm going to party!" Lily does the samba and everything sambas with her.

"Look at my nails." Sonya moans. "I'll have to get them all redone."

"Hey, Carolina," says Argentina. "Do you have a place to go?"

We all stop and turn, remembering that she's here on her own with no family. She's got a new backpack over her shoulder, and her face has burned a bright red from the desert sun. She oozed confidence these last two days, but now she stands apart listening to us without contributing a word. There's an awkward silence.

"Come over to my place," says Lily. "My mom says there are so many of us she's stopped counting how many plates she puts on the table."

I'm about to say that we could share a room when Carolina starts laughing and shaking her head. "Are y'all out of your minds? After two days with you guys, y'all think I'd volunteer for more time?"

Her face looks even brighter red and her eyes are

gleaming. "Just kidding. Thanks, girls; you're the best. I've got an aunt who lives near Nazareth and she's waiting for me."

The bus chugs to a stop, and the doors wheeze open. "Put your stuff underneath. No bags in the aisle!" shouts Shmulik. He climbs down and opens the storage compartment. "It's your lucky day, girls: you've got the first stop. By the time I make the rounds through the base there won't be a place to squeeze in a scorpion."

I'm about to toss in my stuff when I hear a voice behind me say, "Girls."

That's a voice we'd recognize in our sleep. Snapping to attention, we turn around.

Our commander is standing there in her tightly pressed army fatigues. As usual, not a hair is out of place and not a hint of a smile slips through her steely countenance.

"Something's come up. We need eight extra girls for guard duty tonight."

"Now?" says Sonya. "But we're done. You said we could go home."

Our commander doesn't answer.

We look at one another, waiting for someone to clear up this mistake. We'd come for one night, not two.

"Can she make us stay?" asks Argentina.

"It would be on a voluntary basis," says our commander.

"I wouldn't mind, but my boyfriend's waiting for me," says Noga. "At the bus depot," she adds, holding up her phone. "I have to see him. It's been over twenty-four hours."

"My chickens," says Pigtails. "I didn't arrange for anyone to feed the animals tonight. I thought I'd be back."

Lily huffs. "I can't believe this."

"If there is a problem, Lily," says the commander, "I can't force you to stay."

"No problem, Commander. My mom is going to wonder why I didn't get back, that's all."

"You have a cell phone. Send her a message. One of you can go, though."

We avoid looking at one another.

"Sarah should go," I say, breaking the silence. "We're all planning to go home and relax. She's got those chickens counting on her."

"Thanks, Aggie," she says. "Honestly, I would stay—"

"It's okay," says Sonya. She sighs. "Really, my nails can wait another day."

Shmulik climbs back on the bus and revs the motor. "Hey, girls, lighten up. I'll be back tomorrow to come get you."

Sarah throws her bag inside and climbs on.

We don't move.

Shmulik slams the bus doors closed—with us on the wrong side.

"He's really going," says Hadas.

"Without us," says Argentina.

"My mom is waiting for me," says Amber. "No one told us that we might have to stay an extra night."

"There goes freedom." Lily groans. "Smelling like a stinky city engine, spewing out black smoke, and growling like it's on its last legs."

"Somehow," says Argentina, "it feels a whole lot worse to lose something you didn't even know you had until it is taken out from under you."

"Snatched," Hadas corrects her. "Snatched before you realize how much it means not to be able to go home when you were told you would be able to."

"Freedom." My voice cracks. I watch enviously as the bus pulls to the next stop outside barracks nine through twelve and a bunch of soldiers, laughing and jostling one another, fight to get on first and secure seats. One of them is surely Noah. He's going home for a twenty-four-hour leave, but I won't get to see him. I can't believe this is happening.

"Snatched," says Hadas, kicking at one of the lime-covered stones.

"Snatched," we agree, and lug our duffel bags back to the barracks.

Chapter Ten

"It's open!" Shira's mom calls as I raise my hand to knock on the door.

I walk into the hall and almost trip over a pair of scruffy, red army boots. A rush of adrenaline wells inside me.

Noah. He's home!

"Come on in, Aggie." Shira's mother pokes her head out of the laundry room, which is at the far end of their kitchen. "You kids have gotten so busy lately. I don't think I've seen you since Passover. How was your holiday?"

"Fine, thanks," I say, glancing at the piles of army-issued uniforms, gray socks, and clothes in heaps that litter the floor, waiting for their sergeant to move them from one strategic point to the next. Wash, rinse, dry, fold, and back into army kit bag until the next operation.

"Shira had a wonderful time celebrating the holidays with her cousins in the States—though she missed you." Then with a smile, as if noticing my impatience to run upstairs, she says, "Go on. I'm sure you've got a million things to catch up on." She empties a few loose bullets out of Noah's army uniform before tossing his pants into the washing machine. "Noah's home, too," she adds, her voice singing the words as if they're the refrain of her favorite song.

I dash upstairs and tiptoe past Noah's room, where guitar strumming drifts through the partially open door. My toes are tingling, as well as other parts of me.

It's not that I'm holding my breath; I've just stopped breathing.

"Hey, Aggie," he calls, just as I think I've made it past his room unnoticed. I step back and smile at him from his doorway.

"Oh, you're home," I say, as if the sight of his army boots, his kit bag, his clothes strewn across the floor next to the kitchen, and the smells of all his favorite foods cooking had escaped my notice. "I didn't know you were here."

"I'd like Shira to hear you say that." He laughs softly and hums a bar of the piece he was just playing. "She complains that when I come home the whole world starts revolving in Noah orbits." He dimples at me. "Come on in to Planet Noah. I'm only here for twenty-four hours—and half of it's already gone. I was hoping you'd come by." He pauses. "I was sorry that I missed seeing you after your boot camp. I've been wanting to hear how it went."

Taking a tentative step in, I'm not sure how to stand, wishing my commander were around to order "at ease." I lean against the wall next to his dresser, which is piled high with guitar music, clothes, old school textbooks, used batteries, a model airplane kit, and other odds and ends. He's watching me. It takes all my self-control not to fidget as his eyes skip over me, taking in the frizz in my hair to the laces of my shoes. I tug at the end of my shirt, noticing how his glance pauses on the slip of skin between the hem of my top and the belt of my jeans.

Quickly he averts his gaze and strums his fingers across the strings. He's sitting on his bed, back against the wall, legs stretched out, wearing blue sweatpants and a faded button-down shirt that's mostly unbuttoned. A wet towel hangs over the edge of his bed, and soap smells linger in the air. I want to stay but don't know if I've already stayed longer than I should.

"Shira?" I manage to say, my voice sounding like a chord played on the wrong frets. "I haven't seen her since she got back."

"On the phone," he says, which we both know means that she'll be talking for at least another half hour. "Have a seat."

Where? Panic. On the chair that's covered with clothes? On the floor? On his—*ohmigod*—bed?

Sensing my hesitation, he looks around, notices the mess, and I think he almost blushes as he whips his bedspread up over the wet towel and other stuff, shoving it all aside to make room for me on the clean white sheet tucked around the corner of his mattress.

I sit so far on the edge that I almost slip off. I stub my foot on the butt of his rifle, which is only half under his bed, and just catch my balance before making a total idiot of myself.

"Listen," he says. "I think I've perfected the picking on this song." He glances up at me with his soft hazel eyes, and I try to meet his look without wavering and not showing how I've totally lost control on the inside, where pulses beat, blood rushes chaotically, and my emotions have declared a state of anarchy.

He folds up his legs to make room. I scuttle back

a bit, trying to get comfortable while keeping enough space between us. I can't stop looking everywhere. The book he's reading lies on the floor spine up. Twisting my head, I can just read the title, *On the Road*, and there's a picture of a guy leaning on a wall and smoking a cigarette. Another guitar in the corner is missing three strings. Crumpled pieces of paper litter the floor around the wastepaper basket. I want to take it all in. This is Noah, I think. The smell in his room is of worn clothes, oil rags for his gun, shoe polish, and shampoo.

Get a grip, I try telling myself.

"Do you know it?" he asks.

"Know what?" What did I miss? Has he asked me a question?

"The song. 'April Comes She Will.'" He starts to play, singing softly, his eyebrows reaching upward as his voice stretches to meet the high notes.

But April is already gone, I think. And so has March. And it's already June, and this is the first time we've been alone again since you kissed me. Have you forgotten? Does it mean the same thing to you that it means to me?

His fingers move deftly along the neck of the guitar, a team of acrobats leaping from one position to the next. And just like the spectators at the circus, I gape in rapt suspense, my heart soaring and lunging with each move.

"Well?" He glances up at me, almost as if expecting my approval.

"Well what?"

"Did you like it?" He laughs. "You're daydreaming."

The blood rushes to my face. "Music does that to me sometimes," I say, feeling oh so adolescent.

He chuckles softly. "Me too." Stretching his legs, he accidentally brushes my thigh, moves his foot aside without saying a word, looks at me as if he's forgotten the words to the verse he's been singing, and returns to the chorus.

I get up and move to his window. Shira will be off the phone any moment and will start yammering away at me about the Statue of Liberty, Staten Island, and all of Victoria's secrets. My thoughts are running so quickly that I don't realize the music has stopped until I feel his presence so close to me, my skin tingles.

"New moon," he says.

"Where?" A big lemon tree in his yard obstructs my view.

Placing his hands on my shoulders, he tilts me sideways. "Up there."

I look upward. He bends forward and rests the very

tip of his chin on the crown on my head. "Beautiful, isn't it?"

"Yes," I say, though my eyes are closed.

"You're trembling."

"Chilled," I answer.

I hope he'll slide his arms around me and pull me tightly against him. But instead he takes a step back. I turn, the moon forgotten. He hands me one of his sweatshirts.

Slipping it over my head, I am suddenly engulfed in Noah. His smell. The maroon red of his sweatshirt reaches down to just above my knees. The sleeves swallow my hands. My hair is trapped within the collar but for a few unruly frizzes that break free.

"It's you," he says.

I move to catch a glimpse of me in the mirror, but it's the reflection in Noah's eyes that holds me, making me feel like Miss Universe. The paratrooper's emblem is emblazoned across my chest, and though my feet are still grounded on the floor, inside I am soaring.

"We never got a chance to talk about . . ." He pauses as if to gather his thoughts. But I am in a hurry to hear. Shira will burst in any moment. His mother will call him. He'll have to rush out and return to the army.

"What?" I almost shout, the suspense too pressing to restrain.

"Boot camp?"

"Oh right," I say, trying to recall, but my mind is focused on the kiss and doesn't he want to talk about that.

Before I can answer Shira barges in, throwing the cordless phone on the bed. "We need another line!" she hollers. "Call waiting, call waiting, call waiting, every two seconds. How's a person supposed to have a normal conversation when you're around?"

Noah looks at her and blinks. "Who called?"

"Who called? Who didn't call? Lital called three times. Donna called twice. And when Ella called, I told her to take a number and that you'll get back to her whenever."

Somewhere between when Shira started hollering and now, Noah has retreated to his spot on the bed. His head bends forward over his guitar so that just the spiky buzz of his hair is visible and tiny specks of red on the tips of his ears.

"Come on, Aggie. Let's go. I just got off the phone with Ron. They're going to meet us downtown."

She drags me out of the room as the phone starts ringing.

"What are you wearing?" she says, tugging at the sleeve of Noah's sweatshirt. "Tell me you aren't going out in public in that thing!"

I look back, wanting to see Noah's face when he answers Lital's, or Donna's; or Ella's call. The phone keeps ringing, but he doesn't pick it up, doesn't toss it aside, just goes back to his guitar as if he doesn't even hear it.

I grab the door jamb as Shira tugs me again. "Bye, Noah," I say.

He looks up. His lips part as if I've just said something to amuse him, and his eyes catching mine are steady. "Bye, Aggie. Have fun tonight."

Shira gives me a strange look. "What's that all about?"

"Nothing," I say.

"Nothing," she repeats. "Noah," she mutters as she slams the front door behind her. "He thinks the world revolves around him."

And I'm thinking, Yes, I could see why that would happen.

Though it's getting kind of old, we still meet at the same spot. Cat's Corner. Shira has insisted I lose the sweatshirt, so we're both shivering in our skinny tops while we wait for Ron and Ben to show up.

"It feels like a million years since we've had a chance to talk," says Shira. "I haven't even shown you my pictures from the States."

"I know. So much has been going on."

Shira giggles. "And you've been holding out on me!" She puckers her purple lips and mimes a kiss. "Why didn't you tell me?"

"What?" My heart skyrockets. He told her? Confided in her? I want to grab her and shake out every detail. How did he look when he said it? Was he laughing? Serious? The fact that he even mentioned it! My mind races forward with a zillion questions.

"What did he say?" I ask, cringing in case it's not what I want to hear.

She laughs and mimicks the expression on my face. "Well, Ron didn't go into all the details."

"Ron?"

"Yeah. He told me that Ben was all excited about it, as if it was meant to be. The four of us being friends—"

"What?" I realize that Shira has it all wrong. "No, no. It was one kiss! Come on, Shira. It's Ben we're talking about."

She looks at me suspiciously. "Yes, Ben." She pauses. "I thought you'd be thrilled." She shakes her head and shrugs. "I've only been away for a few weeks, but between my trip, singing lessons, you and your boot camp, and Ben and Ron going into the army, it's like we've all morphed into different people."

I have to tell her now, or she'll never forgive me. Ben and Ron will be here any minute. I can't have her thinking that I'm crazy about Ben when it's Noah I miss and I've only left him a few moments ago.

"Shira?" I shiver as a breeze of Jerusalem air slips under my shirt.

"Where are they already?" She stomps her feet to keep warm. "I'm freezing. Summer. Ha! You'd think the nights could warm up a bit."

"Listen—"

"Hey!" shouts Ben, walking toward us. He stops a few meters away and takes an army stance. "Well, what do you think? See any difference?"

Shira giggles. "Show-off. Yes, we see that you are on the way to becoming a Navy SEAL—with the ego of a whale," she teases.

Ron laughs. "You've got that right."

I give Ron a quick hug. "Congratulations," I say.

"Aggie?" says Ben. "I'm waiting."

"You look great, too, Ben." I give him a quick hug.

"Is that all?" he asks.

"Your dad must be thrilled."

Ben smiles. "He sure is." He moves toward me, but I've already linked arms with Shira. He gives me a puzzled look. I smile and shrug.

"Where should we go?" I ask, my voice too cheerful.

"I saw a bunch of guys from my unit hanging out at the square and said I'd take you girls over to meet them."

"Great," says Shira.

We cut through the narrow passages, passing bars, restaurants, bookstores, and tourist shops. "I could use a pizza," I say, getting a whiff of melted cheese.

"Still serious about getting into that combat unit?" Ben tweaks my hips. "I'd say there's at least another inch here since the last time I checked."

I slip out of reach.

"You better watch it, Ben," says Ron.

"Aggie," says Shira, "you are the only person I know in the whole world who wants to put *on* weight." She looks at me with exasperation. "I wish I had such problems. Being on the stage, I have to be careful about every crumb I put in my mouth."

Ben steps in front of us. Pulling me away from Shira, tugging me closer to him he says, "I've missed you."

I press my palms against his chest to push him back. "Ben, wait."

"Hey, don't be so mean. This is the last time I may be able to find your waist. Next time I might need a team of excavators to dig through the levels."

"Ben!" says Shira.

He chuckles. "Just teasing. Even with a little extra meat, you'll always be my Aggie."

He gets the laughs he's looking for, and sliding his hands from my waist around my back, holds me even closer. "School's out," he whispers. "Exams are over. Military life is here. We've got a lot to catch up on and no time to waste. Let's relax and have some fun." He nuzzles my neck and groans. "You smell great."

"It's just Shira's jasmine perfume," I mumble, thinking of how Noah had looked at me in the desert though I smelled of sweat and desert dust. And how, just moments earlier, Noah made my pulse race as the scruff of his unshaven face prickled my scalp.

"Hey, you two," says Shira, smiling knowingly. "We're in the middle of the pedestrian mall—where people *walk*. You might want to move aside and let them pass."

Ben releases me from his grip. The four of us get swept up in the crowd until we reach the square, where a motley group of musicians is jamming. Bongos, guitars, and wooden flutes draw us in. Three girls in long skirts and hair to their waists are dancing.

"I'll go find the guys," says Ben.

The music pulses inside me. My hips sway. My feet pick up the rhythm. "Shira," I say, wanting to confess and tell her everything. Tell her that though Ben isn't right for me, I still want us all to stay friends.

"Don't you love it?" she shouts over the music. "I could stay here forever. Freeze time so that nothing would ever change."

But things have changed, I want to tell her. We've changed. I slide over to her. "I've got to tell you something. It's important." But just then, over the beating of the drums, I hear someone calling my name.

"Aggie!"

It takes me a moment to recognize her, but when I do, I break into a run, and we meet in the center of the square and throw our arms around each other like long-lost sisters.

"Hadas, you look so different. I almost wouldn't have recognized you. What happened?"

North Carolina has exchanged her boots and army uniform for open-toed sandals, low-riding jeans, and a ribbed shirt that reveals a shoulder full of freckles. Her hair hangs loose, and like a sunburn turned to tan, some of her bewildered innocence seems to have faded.

"You look—you look so Israeli!"

We laugh and hug again. I catch Shira watching us, and I pull away from the music to where we can all talk.

"Hadas and I were in boot camp together." I introduce her to Shira. "Have you heard anything yet?"

Hadas shakes her head. "I think it's still too early."

Ben and Ron see us and come over. "Hadas has just immigrated here from the States," I explain. "We met in boot camp."

Ron's mouth drops open. "Really?" he says.

Hadas looks at him, raises an eyebrow, and glances back at me.

I swallow back a giggle. "What are you doing here?" I ask her.

"Good question," says Shira. "What *are* you doing here?"

"Taking Hebrew classes. I also have all these bureaucratic things to do for my immigration status." She groans. "It's such a hassle."

"Then why bother?" asks Shira.

"Do I have a choice?" asks Hadas, her tone and pitch mimicking the well-worn phrase.

Ron laughs. "She says it without even an accent."

"No choice?" Shira interrupts. "Manhattan or Jerusalem." She pretends to weigh the options in the palms of her hands. Her right hand, the one with the silver rings, sinks with the imaginary weight.

"She's teasing," I say. I want to take Hadas's hand and squeeze it, tell her she doesn't have to defend herself in front of my friends. "Shira wants to be the next music diva of the Middle East. After she's conquered Jerusalem she's headed west."

Shira makes a face at me. I'm talking too fast, trying too hard. This meeting of my two worlds is unhinging me. "We were just going for coffee," I say, sure that if Shira gets to know Hadas, they will find so much in common. "Want to join us?"

"Only if you're going to add a big slice of chocolate cake to your order." She lets her eye slide over me and frowns. "You haven't been doing your homework." She shakes her head.

Shira groans.

Ben snakes his arm around me. "Aggie realizes that

you have to have a bit more than a chunky waist and a passing whim to be a soldier in our military. What we do is serious stuff." His chest puffs out. "You got to have the right genes."

"That's exactly what the girls said about her," says Hadas. "Aggie's just like her father."

I bristle. I didn't know they had been talking behind my back. "What's that supposed to mean?"

Shira closes ranks with me. She knows that Hadas has hit a sensitive spot. My dad's shadow could wilt a valley of sunflowers.

"I never met him," says Hadas. "But the girls say your dad can move mountains, and that it was obvious from the way you handled yourself in the field that you are going to do it, too—sandbag by sandbag." Hadas rises onto her toes and laughs. "You should have seen her out there in the field."

I catch the look on Ben's face as Hadas goes on about me.

"Really?" says Shira.

"Honest. She was amazing. Not to mention that the two of us had the best V formation."

She turns her heels into a perfect ballet first position and snaps to attention.

"At ease," I say. "Some of those sandbags were the easier ones to move," I add, thinking of how everything is becoming so complicated.

"Don't I know it," says Hadas. "My mom's mailed me a return ticket." She pats her pocket.

"So what about that coffee?" says Ron.

"Thanks, but not tonight. I'm here with my Hebrew class, if you can call it that. I think I'll end up learning more Russian and Spanish. I never even knew there were Jews in some of those places." She smiles, her freckles scrunching. "And now we're all here trying to cram our heads with a language that looks like an upside-down jigsaw puzzle, all so that we'll understand what our commanders are shouting at us." She shrugs. "My best friend is from Milano and I don't even speak a word of Italian."

Pulling out a book from her backpack, she hands me her copy of *The Alchemist*. "I finished reading it on the bus back from boot camp and have been wondering who to pass it on to. Call me, okay? I'll be here for another few weeks."

"Of course."

"Are you sure you have her number?" asks Ron.

Hadas turns to him. "Why, do you want it, too?"

Ron's face turns red. "Only if you want me to have it." Fumbling for his cell, he rests it in the palm of his hand.

Hadas whispers it to herself in English and then says each number slowly in Hebrew. "Numbers are the hardest," she confesses. "I can't figure out this language gender thing, male and female endings? Instead of Hebrew lessons, they should have sent me for sex education classes."

"I can help you with that," says Ron.

Shira swings around and gives him a look. "Ron—"

His face turns redder than Hadas's hair. "What?" he says. "The Hebrew. I can help her with the Hebrew."

"Right," says Ben, slapping him on the back.

Hadas shakes her head and rolls her eyes. "Well, you've got my number."

She hugs me once more and walks away to join a group of kids hanging out near the bagel bar.

"Now *she* looks like a combat soldier," says Ben.

This time it's my turn to groan. Shira eyes me strangely, and Ron stares off after Hadas as if his Cinderella has run off and he's left holding her army boot.

Chapter Eleven

"Hey, sleepyhead, you have a call"

I roll over, yawn, and stretch. Hadas's copy of *The Alchemist* falls to the floor. I've lost my place. "Who is it?" I mumble, my face squished deep in the pillow.

"Do I look like your secretary?"

I open one eye. Hila is standing at the door of my room wearing a long jeans skirt, a white T-shirt with sleeves to her elbows, and scruffy running shoes. Anywhere else in the world she'd be a fashion disaster.

"No, not a secretary. You look more like the girls who live on the next block across from the synagogue. All you're missing is a book of psalms in your hand and you'd fit right in."

"Thank you. I'll take that as a compliment."

I don't argue with her.

She sighs. "Isn't it about time you've started doing something with these few months left before your draft?"

I pull the blankets over my head.

She grunts disapprovingly. "Well, what should I tell him?" she asks impatiently.

"Who?" I peek out.

She shrugs. "The reception is terrible. It's a guy. Probably Ben, again."

I consider ignoring her and Ben, but instead I pull my quilt over my shoulders and shuffle to the phone in the living room. Curling up on the wicker love seat that once belonged to Grandma, I pull the phone over, wondering why Ben couldn't have called my cell phone and saved me the trip out of bed. He didn't like hearing that what he thought was going to happen wasn't on my "to-do" list before being drafted, and how I thought the timing for us was all wrong.

"Hey," I say, clearing my voice. "What's up?"

Hila walks by and makes kissing noises. I give her a nasty look.

There's static on the line. A couple of crackles. Silence.

"Ben?"

"No, not Ben," says the raspy voice. "Sorry to disappoint you."

"Noah!" My voice, still raw with sleep, croaks. "Where are you?"

"Okay . . . and you?"

My face flushes. "Fine. But I'm surprised to hear from you."

"Good surprised?"

"Of course!"

Crackle. Static. I'm not sure if it's the phone line or Noah thinking of what to say.

"Really?" he says. "And I thought . . ."

"What?"

"Never mind." Static.

I wonder why he's calling me. Shira groans whenever I ask about him. "He's so busy. Doesn't have a second to breathe. He comes home long enough to kick off his boots, throw his uniform in the washing machine, sleep for twelve hours, eat anything worth eating in the house, ask what's up with me, throw one question in about you, and go back to his base."

"About me?"

"Yeah. Always asks if you've heard from the army about where they're placing you—as if you're the first woman ever to get into a combat unit. Do you believe him butting into my life? I've told him more than once to mind his own business."

Laughter. His raspy-voiced chuckle snaps me back. I giggle. Stop. Realize I must sound so childish.

Hila pops her head back into the room, her eyebrows raised.

"What?" I mouth to her.

"Noah?" she says. She smiles and gives me a thumbs-up.

"I'll speak to you later," I tell her, cupping my hand slightly over the phone.

"Call you later?" says Noah.

"No, not you."

"... time so short whenever I see you and we haven't had any time off ..."

More static. I wait, wondering what to say next and what he'll say.

"... never got to tell me about boot camp ... relieved it's over?"

"And how!" This is safe territory, something I can prattle on about and avoid awkward silences. "You saw me after that first night and then they made us stay another one. But at least I had my stuff back."

"... stuff?"

"My bag with all my clothes and toiletries and my sleeping bag got lost the first night and I had to sleep without any of my gear. It was awful! If I hadn't been so exhausted, I probably wouldn't have closed my eyes for a second."

At first I think I hear more crackling on the line and then I realize he's laughing.

"It wasn't funny. I was miserable."

". . . believe they did it to you."

I kick off the blanket and pull my knees to my chest, wrapping my nightshirt over them. I feel snug as Noah's voice sends electric pulses of heat though the phone line. "What do you mean? Did what to me?"

"The missing gear gag. Every group gets one: some poor kid whose gear mysteriously doesn't show up at night."

I press the phone to my ear, struggling to catch every word. "You mean they did it on purpose?"

More laughter.

I imagine Noah's dimples growing deeper at my expense. "That's so cruel! I can't believe they'd do that to someone. I can't believe they did it to me. I was miserable. Why me?" Immediately I think it's Dad's fault. They were testing me—but that's absurd. How could they have known which stuff was mine?

"It's usually the thing that breaks the person," says Noah. "Either you can hack it or you can't and leave. You can learn a lot about a person . . ."

Loud noises, like tanks or something, in the background make it hard for me to hear.

". . . be prepared to deal with all sorts of crap. It's not sleepover camp."

That hurts. "But I didn't break," I remind him.

Silence—static.

"I slept on the ground without even a blanket. Did two guard shifts." I'm trying too hard to impress him but can't stop myself.

"Without even any cosmetics for the next day?" he teases.

Static.

"What?"

"Reception's bad . . ."

"Where are you?" I shout louder.

". . .'p north. Tried calling home but there's no answer."

"Oh." The realization hits me. "You were trying to call home. You're looking for Shira." I'm such a jerk. Of course he's not calling me. If he wanted me, he would have called my cell, not that he has my cell number, but then the fact that he doesn't have my cell number means that he's never bothered to ask me for it—or get it from Shira.

"Yes," he says. "But no," he quickly adds. "I—hello, Aggie? Are you still there?"

"Yes, I'm here." I wrap the blanket back around me.

"... can't hear. Do any of you guys have reception?"

A bunch of male voices in the background are shouting over the grinding noises of tanks and artillery, which makes it even harder for me to hear.

"Noah, I hear you. What do you want?"

"Hello? Aggie? If you can hear me, just wanted to say good-bye. We're going in and won't be able to have our cell phones with us for—jeez, who knows for how long."

"Going where?"

"Oh, now I can hear. We're going into Lebanon ..."

Crackle. Static. "Aggie. Man—I've lost her again. I just wanted to tell you that I— Hey, guys, will you shut up? It's hard enough to hear without all that noise."

It sounds as if a whole battalion of soldiers is in the background gearing up. High, piercing whistles, artillery fire all jar together with shouts and banter. I try and stay focused on Noah's voice, clutching the phone to my ear and barely breathing. "Tell me what?" I shout.

"What?"

There's more laughing in the background. I think I hear my name, then Noah telling them off.

"Noah?" My voice is hoarse. My stomach contracts.

"We've got to go. Aggie, if you can hear me, just wanted to tell you that—I—well—I don't even know if you're still there—but about the other day . . ."

Static. Silence.

"Noah? Noah!" I shout. I'm standing in the middle of the room screaming into the phone. But he's gone.

Mom comes in. She's wearing her baking apron. Her right hand holds a spatula covered in gooey chocolate. Her left cheek is covered in flour. Her face is kneaded into a worried frown. "What's going on?"

"Noah's been deployed, I think. We kept getting cut off. He wanted to tell me something."

"Lower your voice, please. You're shouting."

I catch my breath and realize that I'm clutching the phone as if I'm about to attack someone with it. "What's going on? Why is he going into Lebanon?"

Mom brushes a strand of hair from her face, sprinkling her head with white flour. "I don't know. There have been odd reports on the radio all morning. I've been trying to get your father on the phone but he's been in meetings." She glances over her shoulder to the kitchen, where the mixer is still on.

We avoid eye contact. Mom hasn't discussed the combat issue with me yet. It's not normal. How could she not ask me about it? It's as if she doesn't want to know. Even Noah's asked me.

Noah. My stomach clenches tighter. I imagine him as we walked together to the bus stop, his hands on my shoulders as we searched for the moon. His voice at the end of the line. What did he want to tell me now? That I'll make a great soldier? Or that I shouldn't get the wrong impression about the kiss? The kiss. I touch my lips. I can still taste it even though it's been ages. Can feel the scruff on his chin, the weight of his sweatshirt.

I can't believe I called him Ben.

"Get dressed, Aggie." My mother interrupts my thoughts. "I need you to bring Grandma her eyeglasses. She forgot them here the other day."

The scowl on my face grows deeper. "You never even asked me about boot camp."

I cringe. I sound so whiny. Mom just brings out the six-year-old in me. No wonder she can't imagine me sleeping in the field.

"I have to turn down the oven," she says, retreating to the kitchen.

I follow behind like a toddler wanting attention. It's so humiliating and makes me want to scream. I'm angry. Angry at having called Noah Ben. Angry that I didn't get to hear what Noah wanted to tell me. Angry that Noah has to go into Lebanon and I probably won't get to hear the end of our conversation for another few weeks. Angry that I haven't heard a final answer from the army about where they're sending me.

"Hello!" I shout after her. "I'm about ready to self-combust."

Mom takes a tray of brownies from the oven and puts them on the counter to cool. The kitchen smells of cocoa powder and rising dough. Mom cracks an egg and tosses it into the next batch she's started.

"Do you think that baking yet another tray of brownies will make the fact that I have signed up for a combat unit go away?"

She brushes the flour off her hands. "Really, the way your mind works. Everything somehow reflects back on you. I happen to like baking."

"You bake when you're anxious. A threat of a suicide bomber in Jerusalem, and we've got fresh cookies to last us a week."

"Don't be flippant." She removes the mixing bowl and cradles it between her waist and elbow as she pours it into the pan. She's making enough brownies to feed all of the IDF. Later, that's exactly what she'll do. She'll wrap them up and send them out to all her friends' sons who are serving far from home.

"You thought I couldn't make it and don't want to find out that you're wrong."

She vigorously scrapes the inside of the bowl. "Just the opposite. I never doubted you. So you've definitely passed."

"Yes—" I hesitate.

She looks up, waiting for me to continue.

"I passed the physical endurance tests, but physically I'm—" I stop and have to laugh at the irony of it. "I'm about two brownie trays short of being officially accepted."

Hila saunters in. "What does that mean?"

"I need to gain another couple of kilos by my draft date. Anything under fifty and I'll be disqualified."

Hila snatches a brownie from the tray and hands it to me. "Eat up," she says.

"Wait till it cools." Mom whips away the tray to put it out of reach. "Stubborn mules. You girls have been that way since the day you were born."

Hila and I exchange glances. I'm surprised that Mom is willing to accept that I will do whatever I can to get into the unit, even if it means gaining a hipful of weight.

Hila dips her finger in the leftovers of the bowl of batter

and licks it. "We'll have to start calling you Abundant Aggie. Ample Abigail." She laughs. "I like it." She pokes me in the stomach. "Let's go out for ice cream later. My treat."

Mom's expression is hard to read. Like a familiar book written in a foreign language. I know I should be able to understand it but I can't.

"Are you angry?"

Mom's chest sinks with the depth of her sigh. "Sure I am. I'm angry with a lot of things, most of them beyond my control. Personally, I would prefer if you didn't have to do any army service at all." She eyes me thoughtfully, the spatula in her hand. "But that's not an option. What is an option is where you serve. And frankly, you may as well get it through that stubborn head of yours, you are not going into a combat unit. That just isn't going to happen."

"How can you say that? It is happening. I'm going to make it happen."

She shakes her head. "Aggie, this is serious. Combat is dangerous. You have to be a certain type to be able to cope under very stressful conditions."

"A certain type? If I hear that one more time, I'll scream! What's that supposed to mean? You don't think I can cope?"

Hila wraps her arms around me. "You can cope, as long as you have enough lotion for your sensitive feet. I'll make sure to pack you kilos of it."

"It's not funny."

"Quit teasing her," says Mom. "I'm just worried about what's best for you. You have so many talents, but I don't think you'll find a way to develop them in a combat unit. Think about something more suitable."

"Like an Intelligence unit?"

"For instance."

I sigh. "I have thought about it. But I want to do more than just use my head. I want to move."

"You're too delicate for a combat unit."

"There is nothing delicate about enduring hours of dance class. It calls for muscle strength, endurance, and determination. Mom, I can't sit behind a desk all day. I want to use all of me."

"Except," says Mom, wiping her hands on her apron and looking me over, "there isn't all that much of you, is there?"

"I may be compact," I agree. "But as my friend Lily says, I pack a lot of punch."

Chapter Twelve

I dash for the bus and catch the number 28 just as it's pulling away from the curb. July, and the weather has turned infuriatingly hot, mirroring the frustration bubbling inside me. How does Mom expect me to grow up, take responsibility, stand up for myself, and be somebody if she dismisses me when I finally have my heart set on something and am determined to do what it takes to get it?

I flash my pass at the bus driver and inch my way down the aisle past other sweating bodies. Since Hila's wardrobe has taken a modest turn, she lets me raid her closest. But even Hila's old spaghetti-strap top does little to keep me cool. Strands of hair paste themselves to the sides of my face. I try and pull them back and stick them into a scrunchie. But like an extra layer of clothing, the summer heat sits heavily on me.

Elbowing my way past a group of Ethiopians, I grab a seat next to a woman on her way back from the food market. A huge buggy is parked by her foot, brimming with groceries. Another bag rests on her lap. The smell of coriander leaves wafting from her bag is overwhelming. I think the fish poking out his head from between the leaves, his eye still bright and never losing sight of me, feels the same way.

I consider moving, but the last empty seat has just been grabbed by a woman wearing too many layers of perfume. Don't know which is worse: the botanical garden or tonight's dinner staring up at me. Both smell pretty powerful.

A cell phone starts ringing. The grocery woman begins an excavation to reach the source, her elbow jabbing at my ribs.

"Hold this, darling, for a moment, will you?"

She plants the bag on my lap. Fish to face. I think I'm going to be sick. My stomach clenches. I get up, put the bag on the seat, and smile at her as if the fish needs the seat more than I do.

"Allo, Capara!" she shouts. "I'm on the bus. What's up?"

I grab the pole in the middle of the aisle and stare

ahead, concentrating on holding my balance as the bus lunges and lurches through the traffic.

"What? His left side? Has he been to the doctor?"

I swing along, hoping someplace else will free up and I won't have to listen to the complete medical diagnosis.

"Wait, Capara, I've got another call. Allo? Shimi? I can barely hear you!" she shouts even louder. "Speak up."

The bus lurches to a stop. A seat opens. I lunge for the window and plop down. I've escaped. Tugging the window open, I greedily soak up the breeze.

As the crowd thins and the bus moves on, I get a glance at the leg next to mine—or rather the leg touching mine.

Black jeans. Worn through at the knee. My glance travels higher. He slouches back. One leg stretches into the aisle; the other airbrushes mine. He's solid and muscular. A tight white T-shirt clings to his chest. His hair is gelled into porcupine spikes at the top of his head. He catches me looking at him and grins. He's got bright green eyes set off by his dark skin and high cheekbones. Shifting his weight, he presses his leg just a touch stronger against mine.

I freeze.

He doesn't move.

I've let him invade my space. I should have inched away immediately. Now I'm stuck.

The fish lady groans. "What do you mean you have to go back now? You said they gave you a week's leave. I'm just on the way home—wait a second, Dina's on the other line."

I still could move, but I can't. I stare out the window, pretending that I don't notice that his leg leans against mine, that now his arm brushes my skin.

I struggle between the two mes. The old me would be too embarrassed to brush him off. He probably doesn't even realize that he's sitting so close. The new me? I'm torn between the strange and stirring sensation his touch sends through me and deciding how I should react.

Yoni Rechter starts singing about angel tears. It's one of Hila's favorite songs. I glance forward to the seat in front of me at the lady with the long dark hair blow-dried straight to hang over her shoulders. Her nails are bright red and a small diamond ring is the only piece of jewelry on her hand. She doesn't see me watching her as she flips out her cell phone from the side pocket of her purse.

Black Jeans sighs and stretches. He raises his arm and drapes it over the back of my seat. His other hand rests on his thigh as he taps out some rhythm in his head. I feel the heat of his arm on the back of my neck. Enveloped by his cologne, I feel drugged.

"It's Shimi on the other line. They've called him back. Dina, do you hear me? I've got to go."

"Why do the angels cry?" the cell phone sings.

His thumb brushes the nape of my neck. A rush of tingles sweeps through me. It could be an accident. I think I've stopped breathing. I am supposed to get off in another three stops. I still can't move.

"But I'm just on the way back!" shouts the fish lady. "I've bought sea bass. It's your favorite."

"Allo, sweetheart," croons the lady with the straight hair. "I'll be home by five o'clock."

"And everyone's coming! Yossi, Avi, and his wife, the twins. Avi got a new job at the post office."

". . . the red dress." She gives a throaty laugh. "I bought it especially for tonight."

He hitches his thumb between the spaghetti strap and the hollow by my collarbone. That can't be accidental. His thigh presses harder against mine. I stare forward, feeling my heart jumping inside me. Hila would be appalled. Shira would roll her eyes and tell me how it happens to her all the time. Lily—don't know why she popped into my head, but—I can see Lily turning around and giving him something to remember her by. Ben would get a kick out of it. And I'm thinking, Why me? What is it about me? My clothes? If I were wearing an army uniform, would he dare?

I scrunch closer to the window. His thumb hooks tighter around the strap of my shirt.

"What do you mean?" says the lady, smoothing back a wild strand of hair. Her tone has turned petulant. "You said we'd have the whole weekend."

A song by Snakefish starts up. A soldier at the front of the bus digs into the thigh pocket of his uniform.

Black Jeans places his palm flat on my shoulder, gently fans open his fingers, and reaches across the base of my neck.

"Now?" says the soldier, cupping his hand over the speaker of his cell phone.

"The fish will smell like skunk by then."

"What about the wedding? How long are you going for?"

"Yes. I'm on my way to base now."

The whole bus begins to ring, sing, and vibrate.

A strong, throbbing beat from the pocket of Black Jeans pulses against my leg. Reluctantly he pulls back his arm. I exhale and quickly take a breath in case I'll need to store up more air for later. He reaches into his pocket and pulls out his cell phone. He shoots me a sideways glance before flipping it open. The trance music stops.

Trance. It figures.

"Allo?" He straightens and bends forward. Glancing at his watch, he nods his head as he listens. "When?" he asks. "Now? Of course." He shoots me a sideways glance. "No. Nothing I can't pick up later." He smiles knowingly.

And then that's it. I've had it. As if responding to my cue, I stand up and brush past him. "Think again," I say. "You won't be picking up this one later."

He cups his hand over the speaker, smiles, and shrugs as if to say it was fun while it lasted.

I move back to my old seat, preferring the company of the slimy fish.

More phones start ringing.

The buzz on the bus is contagious until I realize that my phone is jumping in my pocket. I put it on vibrate before I went to sleep last night, and now it's hopping about like a frog hyperventilating.

"Mom? What's up? I haven't reached Grandma's yet. The traffic is awful." My cheeks feel hot, sure that she has psychic powers and knows what's just happened.

"Come home," she says.

"What? Didn't you hear me? I said I haven't gotten there yet. It'll take another twenty minutes at least."

"Now," says Mom, and hangs up.

The bus brakes to a stop before the next official stop. The driver gets up, picks up his bag, takes his phone, hitches his sunglasses onto the crown of his head, pockets his newspaper, opens the door, and walks off the bus.

"Allo?" the fish lady shouts by my ear. "And what about us? How are we supposed to get home?"

The four Ethiopian women, speaking in Amharic, singsong their confusion. I don't understand the words, but I feel the same. Leaning out the windows, we watch the bus driver as he exchanges a hug and handshake with another driver who gets on in his stead.

Our new driver readjusts the mirror, fiddles with the seat, and glances back at us. "He's been called up."

And then we all look at one another: the woman with the fish, the perfumed lady, the soldier at the front of the bus, the religious man glancing up from his open prayer book, the Arab guy reading a library book, and the drop-dead gorgeous guy who minutes ago had his body language all over me and who has just morphed into someone much more serious.

The radio on the bus beeps the hour. We already know what the first broadcast will be.

"Israel Defense Forces are being deployed along the Lebanese border as tensions flare and the Syrian-backed Hezbullah shoots rockets over the northern border. Reserve soldiers are being called up . . ."

We don't have to hear the rest. The bus driver opens the door at the next stop. I get off and get on the next bus going back—only this bus is eerily silent. We've all gotten the message, and even those who haven't yet, know how to read the signs.

It's war.

Chapter Thirteen

After running down the last hill, I hop our stubby stone garden wall, snatch a handful of ripe apricots from the tree outside our house, and take the steps two at a time. The door to our house is propped open to let fresh air in and the cooking smells out. Mom has the radio on in the kitchen and doesn't hear me come in. Hila's backpack is missing from the entrance. There's no sign of Dad either.

"Mom?"

"In here."

I follow the smell of sautéing onions. "Got these for you," I say, putting a handful of ripe apricots on the table.

"Thank you," she says without turning from the stove.

"Where's Hila?"

She doesn't answer.

"Mom?"

"Her group was sent north to help out at one of the old people's homes."

"For how long?"

She shrugs her shoulders. Her head stays bent over the frying pan. "In the last few hours, five rockets have fallen in the area."

I understand Mom's reluctance to talk about it, but I have to know. "Did anyone get hurt?" I pause. "Will Hila be okay?"

Mom mixes the onions. "Hila says that half of the old people are too deaf to hear the warning sirens that go off before the rockets fall. The other half who hear are too confused to understand what's going on, and none of them are able to go running down to the bomb shelters fast enough." Mom brushes off her onion tears. "I think they'll move the whole place underground until this passes."

Until this passes. I take a deep breath and exhale, not brave or stupid enough to ask how long that will be.

Mom wipes her cheeks with her sleeve. Onion skins litter the counter and the floor beside her feet. I scoop them up and toss them in the trash.

"When's Dad coming home?"

Mom slices the mushrooms. "Not for a while." With a practiced swoop she slides them into the pot.

"He hasn't been called up, has he?"

Mom shakes her head. "Not to the front lines. But it seems they need people with his experience." She scoops up a bunch of parsley, rinses it, and starts chopping.

"So what's all the food for?"

"Your cousins from Haifa are on their way. They're going to stay here for a while until the situation quiets down."

"Oh." I take this news as a sign that for all of us life will have to adjust. Dad's been called to help. Hila's gone north. Mom's cooking up a storm. The cousins are coming. I feel useless.

I leave Mom to her vegetables and the radio playing the songs from the sixties, seventies, and eighties between news updates. I go to my room and shut the door. I'm not sure what I'm going to do, but I know that somehow I will find a way to help out.

The next morning I wake up to my phone beeping in a message. It's from a number I don't recognize.

Rocket landed in our bathroom. Holy Sh–t! Place is a mess. But we're all fine. Lovin' Lil.

I call back.

"Hey Sugarpear, what's up?"

Lily's voice makes me laugh. I imagine her full-lipped smile, her dark mascara-framed eyes, and her streaked eggplant hair.

"I just got your message."

She laughs. "Yeah, it's all pandemonium here—hang on—oops."

There's a crash. My heart jumps. "Lily? Are you okay?" I strain to make sense of the muffled indistinguishable sounds. Missiles? Gunshots? "Lily!"

"Yeah, yeah. I'm here. Sorry. I've got my hands full of couscous, and I dropped the phone in the *kubbe* meat."

"*Kubbe*? What's going on?"

"Putting you on speakerphone while I cook!" she shouts. I hear what sounds like rocket fire, but then it could be a metal spoon against a mixing bowl. "My cousin Rita's getting married to this sexy Kurdish guy."

"Congratulations, I guess." I listen to the background noises of voices, cutlery, and pots banging. "And she's getting married—now?"

"Crazy. I know."

I hear more short bursts of gunfire. "Lily?"

"Just banging a spoon," she says. "Anyway, it's not like Rita doesn't have a lot going for her."

Lily's voice gets muffled again. She's either cracking sunflower seeds between her teeth or chewing on a carrot.

"Mom says the problem is that she's too choosy. So now that she's agreed, well"—more bangs and strikes—"my aunt's afraid to wait in case Rita changes her mind. Mom's got everyone rolling *kubbe* balls, and I've made enough couscous and soup to last a century."

"But when the sirens sound, you go into the bomb shelters, right?"

Lily laughs. "Of course."

I don't know whether I want to laugh or cry. "Can I help?"

"You want to roll *kubbe*?" She snorts. "You don't know the first thing about *kubbe*."

"I could—"

"Water!" someone shouts. "My hands are sticking. Bring water!"

I can almost smell their kitchen. See the soup bubbling in the pots. "I feel so useless."

"Well, hey," says Lily, "there's always some way to help."

I tuck the phone between my ear and shoulder and pull my backpack from the closet. "Anything."

"We've got all these strays."

"Strays?"

"Abandoned animals. Poor things. One second they're being petted, pampered, and fed, and the next, their owners have skipped town."

A surge of excitement rushes through me. I'm going. I don't know the first thing about rolling *kubbe*, cooking couscous, or catching strays, but I do know that I'll do anything to help. I stuff my sweatshirt in my bag and throw in an extra pair of sweatpants.

"The dogs," says Lily. "They hear the rockets even before our radar system picks them up."

"Really?"

"Yeah. They start moaning and howling, and before anyone can figure out what's wrong, the warning sirens are blaring, their owners are running around like the dogs have rabies, and then, splat, a rocket lands in the middle of their dinner dish and it's raining doggie dinner bites."

"Or it lands in the toilet," I add.

She doesn't answer. "Mom says she's always hated the tiles in the bathroom and it was time to get it renovated. We're living with my aunt for now."

"Crowded?"

"Think of all us girls in that tent and then add a few

rowdy uncles, a bunch of obnoxious cousins, and three meals a day interrupted by air raid sirens."

"Insanity," I say.

She laughs.

I toss Hadas's book in my bag, thinking that maybe Lily or somebody will want it. What else? I've never lived in a bomb shelter and am not sure what I'll need. I throw in a deck of cards and a nail file.

"What are you doing with the animals?"

"Petting zoo at the hospital."

"And the patients?"

"Oh, they're there, too. It's like those sick kids are the only sane people around. They have this kind of 'whatever' attitude to life, you know?"

No, I don't know. But I'm ready to go and find out. Hairbrush. A few more pairs of underwear and socks. I hadn't really imagined rounding up stray animals, but it figures that Lily would think of the things that other people overlook: stranded animals, sick kids.

"Which bomb shelter are you using?"

"The biggest one."

"Where's that?" And then before she can answer me, I hear a loud, blaring siren. "Lily?"

"This next batch will have to wait—"

I hope she means the next batch of *kubbe* and not the next batch of missiles. "Lily—"

The phone line goes dead. I press send. Nothing. I hold the phone outside the window. Push send again. Nothing!

"What's the good of modern technology," I holler, "when it doesn't work when you need it?"

"What?" Mom yells from the kitchen. "Did you call me?"

I grab my bag and stomp into the kitchen, where Mom is still cooking and organizing.

"What's that?" says Mom. She's holding a sharp knife and jabbing it in the direction of the bag on my shoulder.

"I'm going up north to help out."

"I don't think so," she says. Her voice is strangely calm. She leans against the counter and looks me up and down. "You will stay right here where I know where you are and how you are." She reaches for a tomato and slices it down the middle with one swift karate chop. "You haven't even eaten breakfast.

"Thanks, but I'm not that hungry now."

"Have a sandwich," she says.

"I said I'm not that hungry. But thanks."

"You're not going."

"What do you want me to do here?" I ask her.

"What are you planning to do there? Unlike Hila, you go green at the sight of blood."

"I won't be patching up any wounded. I'll be helping the abandoned animals."

"Animals? We've never even owned a dog. What do you know about animals?"

"I've walked Benz."

Mom snorts and wipes her face on her sleeve. "You're being ridiculous."

We both jump as the front door slams shut. Grandma strides into the kitchen, smelling like lilac and ashtray. She's toting an overnight bag.

"Hi, Grandma." I give her a kiss. "You can have my room. I'm going up north."

"I said you're not going anywhere."

Grandma looks at each of us. Mom turns back to the stove. The only sound is the soup broth bubbling on the stovetop. Grandma knows she's entered a war zone. Reinforcements, I think. Just in time.

"Grandma? Tell her, please."

"Let her go, Eve. Aggie's a smart girl, and while everything's in a muddle up there, they'll need some cool-headed help." She puts down her bag.

"Stay out of this, Tzillah. The world's changed since your day."

Grandma is overcome by her smoker's cough. "Oh, please. Where have I heard that before?" She pours a glass of water. "Eve, you know she has to do this." She takes a sip. "If we aren't impulsive at her age, if we don't believe enough to follow our hearts and act on our beliefs when we're young, then when?"

Mom turns to me, almost pleading. "Don't you understand, Aggie? Before you're drafted, now is the time to live like an ordinary teenager: worried about clothes, your skin, boys, and what movie to watch on the weekend. Soon that will all change. Let us worry about the world for now." Mom's eyes brim with tears. "Enjoy this time just to be, without having to prove yourself. There'll be time for that later."

"I need a smoke," says Grandma, charging for the porch door.

"Smoking is bad for your health," I call after her.

"And rockets kill you faster," she retorts, "but last time I looked, they didn't come with a warning label."

"You know that's not the same thing, Grandma."

She escapes to the porch and slams the door behind her. My bag rests against my foot.

"It's too late, Mom. I'm going anyway. Being a teenager and worried about clothes, my skin, and which guy likes me: way overrated and not all that much fun. I've got a friend up north who needs me to be with her. That's much more important right now."

"You aren't going," she says. "I forbid it."

I pick up my bag and swing it over my shoulder. "I'll text you a message when I arrive." Turning my back to her, I try to walk with an easy stride that I hope hides the cement block weighing on my heart. I have never disobeyed her like this. I should feel triumphant. But instead I feel a sense of sadness and loss.

I pause with my hand on the door. "I know you still want me to be a kid. But being a kid isn't a luxury I can allow myself now. Maybe if I were living some other life, in some other place. But I am here. And this is now." I make my way blindly to the front door. "Bye, Grandma."

"Aggie!" my mother shouts. "Wait."

As the door slams shut behind me, I realize that I haven't even kissed her good-bye.

Chapter Fourteen

I push my way past the crowds by the ticket desk at the train station in Tel Aviv. Everyone is shouting and shoving one another.

"Nahariya and a return." I stick my head up against the window so the ticket girl can hear me. She looks at me and stops chewing her gum midchomp. It's grape. I can see it and smell it.

"Nahariya, are you sure?"

"Yes. I know where I'm going."

But she's not convinced. Rolling her gum around with her purple tongue, she says, "No one's going that way."

"I am. And I'm in a hurry."

She shrugs and punches out the ticket, takes my money, and then says, "Last train to Nahariya is leaving in five minutes. I gave you a return ticket like you asked, but there may not be any return trains for the next few days." She chews her gum, wraps it around her tongue, and pops a bubble. "In fact, I'm not even sure this train will go all the way to Nahariya. Depends."

"Depends on what?"

She looks at the ceiling and shrugs.

I dash past the crowds all going in the other direction. They're pushing toward the elevators to catch trains going south. No one is pushing to get on my train. When the door shuts behind me, I realize that there's no one else on board this coach but me.

It's a ghost train.

I walk the length of the coach. I have a choice of any seat. I don't have to take the stained one because it's the only free place to sit. Don't have to pretend that the girl sitting next to me chewing her gum and flapping her thighs is not driving me crazy. This has never happened to me before.

In the next coach there's a guy with a computer talking on his cell phone. He has a TV badge swinging from his neck. He looks busy and uninterested in me. I walk to the end, hoping to find someone to sit with.

Empty.

I peek through the doors to the other coach.

There's a load of soldiers in there, lounging on the seats, talking on their cells, and passing around food. They're laughing and joking and look like they're having a great time. I don't go in because I don't belong—not yet. But I'm glad to have them close by—just in case.

Slipping into a seat, I slide over to the window. Put my pack on the empty spot beside me and rest my forehead on the glass. The traffic, like a steady flock of migrating birds, is going south. Traffic going north is about one car every fifteen minutes. I feel like a rebel, and all I'm doing is sitting in one spot. Inside I'm restless, though. Lily hasn't called me back. She might still be in a bomb shelter somewhere. How am I going to find her if her cell phone won't receive calls?

I still haven't eaten and have a sour taste in my mouth. It's fear. I don't know if I have the kind of gumption that Lily has. But then, I'm not sure I'll ever really know how I respond to stress or fear until I'm in the thick of it. How do the soldiers do it? I wonder, peeking through the window into their coach. Most of them have dozed off and are slouched in an untroubled slumber.

They've been trained not to think about it.

I resolve not to think about it. The train speeds

through Binyamina and doesn't even slow down at the station. The platform is empty.

I check out the soldiers again. There's one girl. She's sitting by the window talking on her cell phone. I take a second look at her, trying to imagine myself in her spot.

I think of Lily in her uniform that was too tight and crawling up all the wrong places. I think of me swimming in mine, and all of us complaining about our blistered feet. It's not just that the uniforms didn't fit us—but we didn't fit the uniforms.

And then my mind flashes back to the day before: sitting on the bus beside the guy in black jeans. A jolt goes through me. If I had a bag, I'd throw it over my head. What about when I would be surrounded, the only girl or one of the only girls in a combat unit overrun by guys?

My stomach lurches.

I take another peek into the other coach. The soldier, her hair tied back in a ponytail, is sharing a bag of chips with one of the guys. She looks calm, comfortable, and unthreatened.

It's the uniform.

Like Superman with his cape, Batman with his ears, and Wonder Woman with her breast busters, the

uniforms say "Don't tangle with me; I'm on a mission."
Yes, that must be it.

I jump at the rousing chorus of "We Are Family"
coming from my backpack. I hope it's Hila. Caller ID
warns me that it's Dad.

"Hey, Dad. Where are you?"

"Never mind where I am, where are you?"

I look out the window of the train. Sun rays shimmer
on the water. Now there are no cars on the street. Peering
out the other window, I see the steep rise of a mountain
jutting the skyline. "Around Haifa," I say.

The line crackles, but Dad's voice is clear when it comes
through. "Listen, Aggie, you get off that train right now
and come back home. I don't know what gave you the
foolish idea to go up north but it's too dangerous."

"But, Dad. Grandma said—"

"Grandma? You're listening to Grandma?" He groans
and mutters something under his breath. "Things
have changed since your grandma's time. In her time
she thought all you needed were determination and
dedication and you could change the world single-
handedly. Things are different now, and it's not the right
time to act impulsively. I want you off that train at the
next stop, do you understand?"

The conductor stops by my seat. "Ticket?"

I hand it to him. He punches it and hands it back.

"I need to get off this train," I explain to him. "Where's the next stop?"

The conductor shakes his head. "There isn't one."

I cup my hand over the phone's speaker. "No stops?"

"Well, we're stopping in Nahariya but then that's it. No more trains going either way until things settle down up there."

"So I'm stuck."

He shrugs. "That's about right."

"Dad?"

"This is no joke, Aggie. I want you off that train."

I could try to explain it to him. Tell him to stop bossing me around. Tell him he's wrong about Grandma and that he shouldn't dismiss her like that. She may be old, but some things never go out of style, like determination and dedication.

Dad's still lecturing me through the phone line.

"But there are no . . ."

He won't listen to reason. Won't accept that there is no way to go back. I'm tired of him thinking that I'm incapable of knowing what's right for me. Now is the time, I think, to stand up to him. Remind him that I am eighteen. If that's old enough to be drafted, then it sure must be old enough to decide for myself.

"I'll see if I can get an army car to pick you up," he says.

"What? Hello? Dad?" I grit my teeth and make static noises. "Dad? Can you hear me? The reception's gone. Can't hear you. The train doesn't stop until Nahariya. I'll call you when I get there. Don't worry. I know how to take care of myself."

And then I end the call and shove the phone deep into my bag. Scooping my knees to my chest, I hug them close. Life just keeps getting more complicated, and like the train speeding through the deserted stations in a rush to reach its final destination, I'm not sure what either of us expects to find there.

My telephone beeps in a message. I dig it out, glance at the caller ID, and put it back.

It's Shira. She wants to know where I am. I've forgotten to call and tell her I'm headed up north. Will she understand?

She'll be annoyed that I've gone off without telling her. I groan. One more gibe about the weight thing and I'll scream.

"Girls in combat units," said Ron, last time I saw him. "Sexy but scary."

"I don't think that's why we do it," I answered.

"Watch it, Ron," said Ben. "She's already getting feminist on you."

"I'm not going for combat because I'm a feminist. If you feel a need to carry around my bag with all the equipment in it, hey, go ahead!"

"Backing off," said Ben. "We're backing off."

They didn't ask me why I wanted combat, but I had my answer ready. "Why not?" I mean, if somebody's got to do it, why not me? I think of Lily and her bathroom full of rocket debris. How can I pretend that what happens to her doesn't concern me? That's what I should have told Dad.

I punch in Shira's number. We've been friends for too long for her not to understand.

"Aggie, guess what?" she shouts. Without waiting for me to guess, she sings, "I got it! I got in! I got into the entertainment troop. Isn't that amazing?"

"Amazing!" I answer. "I'm thrilled for you."

"It's a dream come true. I can't remember a time when I didn't see myself in uniform, on stage, lights above, belting out 'Jerusalem of Gold.'"

"I don't think they sing that anymore."

She giggles. "I've been listening to too many of my dad's old records."

This time there's real static over the line.

"Where are you?" she asks.

I explain about Lily, about my dad not understanding, about needing to be a part of what's going on around me. "How do I know if I can hack it if I've never tried?"

I imagine Shira's smile as she clicks her tongue. "Aggie, none of us who know you have any doubt that you'll be amazing, but I know that nothing will convince you until you prove it to yourself. Just take care, okay? Promise you'll call me as soon as you get back?"

"Promise."

The train slows down through Akko. Pressing my face to the window, I watch the restless waves tossing up whitecaps. The palm trees along the coast shiver like they wouldn't mind taking cover or moving to a calmer climate.

By the time the train pulls into Nahariya, I'm still not sure if I'm relieved at having arrived or terrified that I'm really here. The doors swing open. I trail behind the soldiers until the end of the platform. An army transit is waiting for them. They're quieter than when they were sitting on the train. They throw their stuff in, climb on, and take off toward the border.

The TV man is gone, too. In fact, looking around, I see there's no one here at all.

The wind rustles through the trees. The street signs quiver. The traffic lights turn from red to green before switching to yellow. The little green man flashes that it's fine to cross. But there is no one standing on the corner and no cars to heed the traffic codes. No one but me. Standing alone with nothing and no one to protect me.

Chapter Fifteen

I need to head for cover. The community bomb shelter must be near the center of town, I think. I pass a kiosk with an OPEN 24 HOURS sign on the door. It's closed. My stomach grumbles. Anyway, I'm too jumpy inside for a greasy pita filled with oily falafel balls and the spicy sauce that Shira has taught me to eat without gasping for air.

Usually Gaaton Boulevard is teeming with traffic. Today I could stroll down the middle of the street with my eyes shut. Tourist town of the north, Nahariya has boutique shops, coffee shops, cafés, and seaside resorts—only now there isn't a tourist in sight. The streets echo my footsteps. And the air, which on a good day is a mix of overpowering aromas from the bakery, the other falafel stand, and exhaust fumes from the bus depot, is now clean enough to catch a whiff of the sea breeze that blows through the center of town.

What if a rocket is fired right now? What'll I do? Dive behind a car, crawl under a park bench, huddle at an entrance to a building?

I speed up. Mom will never forgive me if anything happens.

I hold the straps of my backpack as I rush on, looking for someone, anyone, to help me. It's so quiet. The kind of quiet that hovers at the base of your neck. A tingling in my toes spreads up through my legs, settling in the pit of my stomach, which is pumping panic.

Nothing in my life has prepared me for fear like this. I catch myself thinking of Grandma. Nothing much ever fazes her. She's been a soldier in a different war and at a different time, but doesn't fear feel the same wherever you are?

I duck into the doorway of the pharmacy to catch my breath. There's an ad in the window for condoms. *Never be caught without protection.*

I look out and hurry on.

At the next block a strange sound catches my attention. I turn the corner and I follow the drone, bang, and thump. I peer around nervously. But it's just a small toy tractor on someone's porch. It races along until it reaches a wall, flips over, turns itself right side up, and races back. I chase after it, looking for who's holding the remote.

But it's on autopilot. Like me, I think. I watch it almost enviously. The way it reaches a wall, flips over, and goes on. No scrapes, no bruises. I hope I'm as indestructible.

After a quick search I locate the remote control and turn it off. At least when the kid returns, he'll find the batteries still working. This street is a residential one. The gardens are well manicured. The houses are quaint and compact. I venture just a bit farther down the block, peeking into the houses, where tables are set but with no one there to eat the food.

It's creepy. I've seen pictures of Pompeii, and even without the lava, this place feels like it's been frozen by an invisible rush of molten fear.

This isn't the right way. I retrace my steps. I am about to rush on when something stops me in my tracks. I strain my ears. It's a cry, like a baby's pitiful whine. Tiptoeing up the path, I see that a door stands ajar.

"Hello?"

The cry grows stronger.

"Anyone here?"

I hover at the entrance, unsure what to do. I can't just walk into someone's house. But there's a baby crying!

Sunlight slips in through the blinds of the window. Like a stage set, the rays illuminate the table where a plastic bowl remains untouched. The spoon is on the floor. A milk bottle is on the counter. A baby bottle! That clinches it. I walk in, grab the bottle, and start searching for the baby.

The crying has gotten softer and turns to a whimper.

I run into a bedroom. Empty.

It takes me a few seconds to locate the source. A baby kitten has crawled onto the highest shelf of the bookcase. He's shivering with fear.

I laugh out loud. Not an abandoned baby, a kitten.

Only then do I realize how loudly my heart has been thumping in my chest. It's just a cat.

"Hey, kitty, kitty. Come on down."

I'm contemplating how to climb up and get it when the front door bursts open. "What are you doing in here?"

I shriek and spin around, terrified by the silhouette of the figure in the doorway. "I heard crying."

He sees the bottle in my hand. "You left your baby here?"

"No. Not mine. Not a baby. I mean—a cat."

He strides in. "You shouldn't be here."

"I—"

"Why aren't you in a bomb shelter? The all-clear signal hasn't sounded."

"I'm not from here. I'm looking for a friend." I hold the bottle tighter. "Lily?"

He groans. I watch him, waiting for what he'll do next. But he's a soldier and not the owner of the house who's caught me breaking and entering.

"You're one of those girls collecting the strays?" He shakes his head. "You're supposed to wait until the all-clear signal sounds before you go out on your rescue mission."

"But I—"

"But you knew that they'd left behind their kitten and thought it couldn't wait. We got a call that there was someone prowling about the empty streets. You're lucky no more rockets have landed."

He sweeps by me. I see his arm is bandaged and swings inside a sling. "Hold the chair," he says. "I'm not that steady."

He climbs up. "Come on, kitty. Let's get you some milk and a safer place to hide out."

The soldier balances on a stool that he's put on top

of the table. As he reaches, his army shirt slides up, revealing the fringes of a prayer shawl tucked beneath his uniform. He coos and finally coaxes the cat inside his sling. "I knew this had to be useful for something."

He passes it to me. The kitten nestles inside my arms close to my heart.

"There. Now, where's your bomb shelter?"

"I'm not sure. Lily said she's in the community bomb shelter."

We walk out of the house. He motions for me to hop into the jeep. I slide in, the kitten snuggled tightly against me—or maybe it's me snuggling up to the kitten.

"That's the shelter near the hotel. I'll drive you over."

As he speeds through the empty street, I sneak a sideways glance at him. His sandy hair is longer than allowed and an inch over the top of his ears. He drives with one hand on the wheel, the other casually resting in his sling.

"What happened?" I ask.

"This?" he says, raising his elbow. He winces. "Shrapnel. It's not so bad. A couple more days and I'll rejoin my unit. For now they've put me in charge of security here."

"Where's your unit?"

He gestures over his shoulder. "Inside." Which I know means inside Lebanon.

There's a pause between us. Silence. And then, taking his eyes for a second from the empty road, he says, "Do I know you from somewhere?"

Shira would roll her eyes and say, "Typical male."

He must realize how that sounds, and stumbling over his words, he hurries to explain. "No, really. I'm serious." He blushes. "Aggie, right?"

The jeep pulls to a stop outside the hotel, but I don't move. "How did you know?"

He laughs. "I'm Jonas," he says, reaching out with his good hand. "Anyone who's spent any time around Noah has got to know who you are."

I'm still speechless and make no move to leave the jeep. "Oh?"

He gets out and walks around to my side. "Are you coming?"

"Wait. How do you know Noah?"

"We're in the same unit. And I don't think Noah would appreciate me chatting with you out here while it's still unsafe. Let's get moving."

"The same unit?" I say, trying to sound casual, but wondering if Noah might be here, too.

"I saw you at the base, when you and a bunch of other girls got back from a field exercise, remember?"

My turn to wince, remembering how we must have looked. I'm amazed he recognizes me without corn in my hair.

"How is he?"

And it's like watching a fade-out on a screen. Jonas withdraws. His smile disappears. He takes a step away from me as if I've invaded his personal space.

"Don't back off. I want to know."

He shrugs. "I don't know what to tell you. Things were okay when I left, but he's in a dangerous place and the situation changes every minute."

I don't press for more information, unsure what questions to ask, unsure that I want to hear the answers. He mutters a name of a village under his breath.

"I hate thinking of them there and me not with them," he says.

Fighting against the tightness in my chest, I turn away from him. But I can't turn my thoughts away from Noah. Here is the front line—but our soldiers have crossed it. I'm outside in the fresh air feeling like I'm suffocating, as if I were already inside the shelter below.

"Really, we shouldn't be standing here," he says.

But bomb shelters are crowded, noisy, and suffocating places, and this one will have a lot of people in it I don't know. I'm scared.

"Anything you want me to tell Noah when I see him?"

My throat is too constricted for me to speak. I can't seem to dig the words out from inside of me. I feel my cheeks getting hot. I stroke the kitten, trying to fight back my tears.

"Okay. I'll describe that for him," he says softly. "He'll want to know everything. It'll give him a lift." He shifts his weight and pulls on the strap of his gun. "I've got to get back to headquarters."

"Can't you stay a bit longer? I really don't want to go into that bomb shelter alone. What if Lily's not there? I don't know anyone."

"Don't worry. You'll feel right at home. During war, we're all family." He reaches out and scratches the kitten behind the ears. "You and your kitten get inside. And Aggie? No more roaming around on your own. Wait until we send out the all-clear signal, okay?"

I nod my head and watch him drive off—but I still don't move.

I hate bomb shelters. I've done enough school drills to know that the ventilation system in the shelter never works well. We'd hoard inside anyway, where usually within minutes we'd be overwhelmed by body odors. And the teachers, fanning themselves by the exit, would look at us with sour expressions on their faces that said that they weren't getting paid enough for this stuff.

But this is not a drill, and I can't continue to stand out here.

I push the door open and step in.

It takes a moment to adjust to the change in light, the commotion of color, and the rush of excitement.

This is not what I expected.

One corner has kids hanging streamers across what looks like a stage made up of overturned cartons with a plywood sheet on top. At the other end of the room an amplifier is being set up and a bass guitar is draped over two chairs. Some vaguely familiar musician-looking types are fighting over the sound system.

I'm wearing jeans and a T-shirt. Everyone else in the room is dressed for the Academy Awards: long-legged, high-heeled women in black beside guys wearing clean jeans and crisp white shirts are mulling about, pausing in front of video cameras to smile and exchange kisses.

Huddling by the wall, I look around desperately for a familiar face.

"Whose side are you on?" asks a soldier suddenly appearing at my elbow.

I blink. It should be obvious. I'm in a bomb shelter. There's no way I can look like a terrorist. "Sorry?"

"You don't look like any of us," he says. His eyes are dark and questioning. He's got a flat nose and swarthy skin. Not too tall and yet solidly built, he seems to have me surrounded just by the bulk of him. He stares at me so intensely, I feel pinned to the wall and inch toward the door, ready to escape.

"His side? Her side?" he asks again.

"Well, I—"

"Ours!" sings out a familiar voice.

And Lily sweeps me into a bear hug. "She's on the bride's side of the family." Lily laughs. "Sugarpear," she says. "What took you so long?"

Chapter Sixteen

"I'm so thrilled you made it," says Lily.

I wipe off my tears, embarrassed to be making a scene. "He must think I'm an idiot," I say, glancing at the soldier who is still watching us.

"Him? That's just Yossi. He's a distant cousin." Holding me at arm's length, she notices the cat. "You brought your kitten?"

"Yes. No. I found it." I gulp. "You won't believe what just happened to me."

Lily shakes her head. "Time for that later. I hope you brought something nice to wear?"

"Sorry, Lily." I blow my nose. I'm still hiccupping as I speak, torn between relief that I made it here and hysteria that I am here. "I guess I imagined you and your family huddled in a damp, cold dungeon with no air and only the sound of chattering teeth waiting for the next rocket to fall." My hiccup turns into a laugh. "I should have known that you'd find any excuse to have a party."

Lily crosses her arms over her chest—which is no small feat—and pretends to look offended. "This isn't just any party. I told you my cousin Rita has finally snagged a guy."

"Yeah, but I didn't think you were serious about going through with it now."

"*Hellz-bollah* if we're going to let some guerrillas with their fingers on a rocket get in her way. The army has agreed to let us hold the ceremony outside once the all-clear signal goes, and then later down here: party time!"

I look around the shelter. "You mean music and dancing?"

"You bet! These guys"—she points to the band—"play in the hottest pubs in Tel Aviv. When they heard we were having a celebration, they insisted on coming here to show solidarity. I said I was hoping that some of them would show us a whole lot more."

"Lily, be serious."

"I am! You can count the number of guys around here who haven't been drafted, and then weed out the cute ones from that, and well, this place should be on a male disaster list somewhere so that they'll fly us in some supplies."

Lily lifts the kitten from my arms and nuzzles nose-to-nose. "I still have a million things to do before the wedding ceremony." She glances at her watch. "Okay, this is what we'll do."

I nod, ready for my instructions.

"I've got a kid in my car—"

"You left a kid in your car?"

She pauses, a look of confusion crosses her face, and then she smiles. "Relax, it's okay."

"On his own? Are you crazy?"

"He's fine. It's a goat, Aggie. Not a *kid* kid." She looks at her cousin Yossi and they both laugh. "If you can take the goat and the kitten to the hospital, it'll save me time."

"You can't come with me?" I ask her. "I don't know where I'm going."

"Yossi will show you the way."

Yossi looks at her. "Lily, I've just got off guard duty."

"You don't have to go in with her. Just point her in the right direction."

"But—I've never driven to the hospital," I say. "I don't know my way around. I don't know the first thing"—I pause—"about goats."

"Goats. Right." Lily holds up her hand to stop my babbling. "First of all, you don't have to worry about navigating through the traffic: there isn't any. The sea is behind you; the hospital, straight ahead. One traffic circle and you're there. Even you don't need GPS for that."

"Very funny."

"Just teasing. When you get to the hospital, circle on back. They had to move the wards underground after one of the wings got hit."

"The hospital was hit—with a rocket?"

"It's okay now, but they're staying underground until things calm down."

Yossi butts in. "We're all wrapped up here together until things calm down."

Lily looks at him and starts fanning the air in front of her. "Talk about being wrapped up together. Are you trying to kill us or something? There's little enough air in this bomb shelter without you puffing on that thing."

He drops his cigarette and stubs it out with his heel. "She's in a bomb shelter worrying about secondhand smoke." He laughs and winks at me. "Dance later?"

"She's busy," says Lily, turning back to me. "The entrance to the kids' ward is on the west side, and someone will know what to do with the animals."

"Someone?"

Lily shrugs. "Aggie, if you made it up here when there's no more public transportation going north and you found me in a city where there is no one to be found, I've no qualms that you'll manage to find the hospital and the kids' ward."

I want to argue, but just then there is a shrill, jerky siren.

"All clear," says Yossi.

"Got to run." Lily throws her car keys at me. "Out back. It's a small Ford Escort. You can't miss it. Sometimes it doesn't want to start, but be patient and keep turning the engine over. The kid's in the front seat."

"Come on," says Yossi. "I'll show you."

Following the crowd, we go back onto the street, which is now bustling with people coming out to breathe. Yossi points out Lily's car. I look inside and freeze. It's worse than I thought.

"Lily!" I scream. "What am I supposed to do with a goat!"

Yossi is doubled over, laughing. "Oh, this is too much."

The goat looks at me, sitting in the front seat as if to

say "What's your problem? We don't have all night."

"Stay here," says Yossi, struggling to catch his breath. "I'll bring my jeep around."

I slip into the front seat and put the kitten inside a little crate that Lily has in the back for transporting the strays. The goat looks back at me, then turns to stick its nose out the window.

"Good," I tell him. "Stay like that and don't do any goat things."

I shift the car into first and pray that it'll start, that I'll make it to the hospital before the next siren sounds, that I'll find what to do with the goat once I get there, and then have time to shower and change in time for the party. I must be out of my mind to have gotten myself into this situation.

Driving behind Yossi, the ride to the hospital starts off as easily as Lily promised. Following the canal that cuts through the center of town, it's impossible to get lost. As we approach the main traffic light that divides everything north on the left and everything south of Nahariya to my right, it turns to yellow. I'm afraid Yossi will barrel through. I'm too well trained to run a red, even if the streets are empty. My luck, I'd hit the one other vehicle on the road—or the one cop car still on patrol. Fortunately, Yossi stops and waits for the green.

The road to the hospital has houses on both sides that now all look abandoned. I try to imagine the place as I've seen it before. Hitchhikers hanging out by the bus stops, scooters weaving through the traffic, and mothers pushing baby carriages along the sidewalks.

We reach the turn-off for the hospital. Yossi waits for me to draw up beside him.

"Sorry, can't take you any farther," he calls out the window. "I've got to get back. Will you be okay from here?"

"No problem," I say with a lot more confidence than I feel.

I drive around the side and leave the Ford in a half-hour parking zone. The hospital windows are all boarded up to protect against shattering glass when the rockets land, giving the place a haunted look. Some of the street lamps haven't been as fortunate, and the sound of splintering glass beneath my feet makes me shudder. I pull the kitten out of the crate and snuggle it in my arms.

"Hey, kitty," I coo. "So far, so good."

Then I stall, wondering how one coaxes a baby goat out of the front seat of a car.

"Baa, baa," I say feebly. "Here, billy goat."

It looks at me, and I swear I think it rolls its eyes.

"Out," I command.

Nothing.

"Please?"

I hear it giggle. Goats don't giggle.

"Who's there?"

A boy, no taller than the goat, crawls out from behind a small stone wall. "Maybe if you pull the string around its neck," he says.

"The string?"

He points to a dangling piece of frayed string. "Pull on it and he'll come out."

"Okay." I have my pride and don't want him thinking I'm afraid of a little goat. I tug on the string, and the thing climbs out. I shut the door quickly—just in case it had any other ideas.

"How'd you know that would work?"

"We've been taking care of the animals that Lily brings here."

I almost say, "Oh you're one of them"—but catch myself in time.

"Aggie," I say, introducing myself. "And you are?"

"Roy."

Roy is short. He's got very fair skin and big round glasses that magnify his eyes. He's wearing a baseball cap, loose-fitting jeans, and a sweatshirt. Not exactly hospital attire, but then goats aren't usually hospital visitors. He has a book tucked under his arm, and his finger inside is marking his spot. He watches me with an amused expression.

"Thanks. I'm not great with—goats. What are you reading?" I ask.

"*The Hobbit.*"

"Yeah? It's good, isn't it?"

"I'm reading it for the second time," he says. "Now I know how Bilbo feels living underground." He stretches out his left arm and shows me his hospital bracelet. "I've even got a ring like he does that can protect me from anything."

"Nice."

He smiles. "Like in *The Lord of the Rings*. I am invincible."

"So you are."

We look at the sky. Somewhere in the distance is the sound of gunfire.

"You're not scared being out here on your own?"

"Sure I am. I'm scared of lots of stuff. But I had to

get out for a few minutes and breathe real air."

Life is strange, I think. The big wars get all the attention while, in fact, so many smaller, private wars are going on at the same time and most of us don't even think twice about them. I look at Roy, wondering what's on his mind.

"My fifteen minutes are up," he says. "Are you coming in?"

"I can't. I promised Lily I'd get back in time for the wedding."

"A wedding?" he asks.

"Her cousin is getting married tonight."

Roy looks at me wistfully. "I wish I could go. I bet there's going to be cake."

I look at him petting the goat, and before I know it I'm figuring out a plan. "Tell you what," I say. "If you take the kitten and the goat inside, I'll be able to make it back for the wedding. And then later, I'll bring you some cake."

"Really?" he says.

"Really."

"You promise?"

"Promise," I say.

Chapter Seventeen

I wait until Roy is safely inside with the goat and the kitten.

I climb back into Lily's Ford and stick the key in the ignition. The engine groans, sputters, and dies. "No. Not now." Turning the key again, I floor the gas pedal. Mustn't flood the engine, I think. It kicks over, threatens to sputter, but I pump the gas stronger and it roars to life.

A glance north and I shift into drive. Rolling out of the gates of the hospital, I breeze through the traffic circle. Like Lily promised, it's a straight ride and only a few kilometers. A piece of cake. Cake. I hope that Lily has found me something normal to wear. I'm actually excited about going to the wedding and think it will be fun to be surrounded by people, noise, action.

Nahariya is so quiet, the air feels heavy with silence. I roll down the window, but hear only the grinding of my wheels on the asphalt. Speeding up just a few kilometers over the limit, I find myself wishing Yossi were driving in front of me. I don't want to get stuck sitting at a red light.

I'm trying to avoid the tingling in my spine. My foot doesn't leave the gas pedal. I'd rather be a moving target than a sitting duck.

I cover another block and allow myself to breathe.

The main traffic light comes into view. It's green. I speed up even faster, racing toward it. The picture of the stickman starts flashing, even though he's the only pedestrian around.

I can make it. The air rushes in through the window, whipping my hair back. Two blocks to go!

And that's when I hear the siren. It starts as a low wail. I ease my foot off the pedal and cast a guilty glance over my shoulder. I was only going a few kilometers over the limit. The road is empty. Just my luck! Pulled over for a ticket the one time—

The low wail starts to build. I check the rearview mirror. There are no other cars on the road. Not even a police car.

Like a tidal wave, the siren washes in from the sea. It rises and shrieks in a deafening blare. Not a police siren—

Air raid!

My stomach clenches. I want to scream, but no sound comes out. I floor the gas.

I hunch forward. Heart pounding in my head.

"Oh no. Oh no. Oh no." My hands grip the steering wheel. My foot crushes the gas pedal into the floor. But where is it? Behind me? What if it's in front of me? Above my head? I duck.

Pressing my chest to the steering wheel, I focus on the traffic light. "Stay green. Stay green."

I pray I will make it to the shelter, to Lily, to safety. I'll make it. I've got to make it.

"Please, please, please," I chant.

Hysteria wells inside of me. I am two meters from the light. It turns to yellow. "No, no, no." I can still make it. "Wait, wait—wait!" More gas. I'm almost there.

Red!

I close my eyes, brace the wheel, and slam on the brakes.

Chapter Eighteen

The car screeches to a stop, skidding over the crosswalk.

The siren is still blaring.

"You idiot!" I scream. "Keep moving, Aggie."

I shift back into first, slam into second. I'm in fifth gear by the time I reach the other end of the intersection. My hands sweat the wheel.

"If I make it . . . if I make it to safety, I will change—for the better, honest."

At the end of the block, I jerk the steering wheel left. Slide into a U-turn, screeching to a halt in front of the bomb shelter.

I kick open the car door. If I make these ten meters, I will never try anything as stupid as this again.

I'm running. But my feet, they're so clumsy. I stumble. Catch myself and hurry on.

If I make these ten meters, I will—

But before I can finish my thought, a shrill whistle pierces the air.

A blast of thunder rocks the ground beneath me.

With meters to go, I am thrown off my feet. I land flat on the earth. My hands shield my head as I press my face to the ground. Around me is the sound of shattering glass as the sky rains window shards.

I lay on the ground, afraid to look around. Have I been hit? Am I safe?

Is it safe now?

The ground shudders. A smell of smoke fills the air. Car alarms blare. I stay pressed to the earth and wait, hands over my head. Is it over?

I listen, too frightened yet to move. My ears are ringing. My head pounds. My whole body shakes uncontrollably.

"Aggie," a gentle voice calls. "Get up. It's okay. It landed in the parking lot. Nobody's hurt."

Lily is leaning over me, stroking my back, pulling me up. Rolling onto my knees, I sit up, throw my arms around her, and start sobbing. "I've never been so scared in my life. My ears. My ears are ringing."

She rocks me in her arms. "It's okay. You're safe."

"What?"

"I said you're safe now."

We stay locked together until my breathing slows and the jarring in my ears subsides.

"I was so scared."

"I was scared for you, too." She helps me onto my feet.

"Is it over?" I ask.

"Until the next time. Come on, Aggie," she says. "Get a hold of yourself. We've got a wedding to go to and you look like one of my soggy strays." She wipes a smudge of mud from my face. "We need to get you accessorized."

I look at her, glance behind me, and start to laugh hysterically. "Accessorized? I was almost pulverized, and you've got earrings on your mind? Lily, you're crazy."

Lily wraps her arm around my waist. My legs wobble. I'm laughing so hard I can't stand straight.

"Come on, Aggie. Get a hold of yourself. We're almost there."

But we aren't headed the right way.

"Shouldn't we be going into the bomb shelter?" I pull away from her, gasping as my laughter turns to sobbing hiccups.

"We should." She smiles. "But the rocket just fell, so it'll take them a while to launch the next one. You need a shower, and I already put the dress in one of the rooms."

"In the hotel? But I don't have a room."

Lily pushes me forward. "The hotel staff is gone, but they've left a few rooms open for those of us whose houses have been hit." She pulls me into the hotel. The marble floors are polished and echo the sound of our feet as we cross the empty lobby.

"How did you know I was on my way?"

She opens the door to one of the rooms and pauses. Turning to me, she smiles and shrugs. "Instinct? I don't know, but I just had a feeling that you were out there and that I had to find you." She laughs. "And then I got a call on my cell phone. And don't you doubt it for a second: our guys know even what color thong you've got on."

I actually catch myself thinking about which one I'm wearing. "What are you talking about?"

"Jonas said he wouldn't let on about the red light, seeing as probably you were scared out of your spaghetti straps— his description not mine—and that it was probably the first and the last one you'd ever run." She pushes me into the hotel room.

"Lily, you're too much."

"Shower," she orders, grabbing the TV's remote control.

"Gladly."

"Make it snappy. We don't have much time."

I help myself to all the freebies: shampoo, cream rinse, body soap, and complimentary body sponge.

I turn the water to maximum heat. The stream is hard and the temperature close to boiling. I want to scorch the fear off of me. Boil, burn, melt it away.

Once out of the shower, I search for my reflection in the mirror that is obscured by the steam. My palm squeaks against the glass as I try to clear a section. But as quickly as I wipe away the vapor, it gathers again and I disappear in the mist. Inside, part of me feels just as elusive. Fear. It's not like I've never experienced it, but this time it was different. Anxiety in the pit of my stomach before an exam, jumping off the cliff of the Judah'ah into waters below, screaming in terror with the exhilaration that comes when losing control: those kinds of fear I've known. But not this.

"Aren't you done in there yet?" Lily calls.

I come out wrapped in a white bathrobe. Lily has dressed in the meantime. Wearing a bright burgundy skintight dress and shoes to match, she could knock out a brigade.

"Well?" she asks, turning around with her arms up.

"You look—"

"Scrumptious?"

"Just the word I was thinking of."

She jumps on the bed. "I'm beat. We've got a few minutes to gather strength before the partying begins." Sitting on the bed with the remote in her hand, she starts flipping channels. "News. News. News," she mutters. "Like sitting in a traffic jam and listening to the announcer say that traffic is backed up all the way to Tel Aviv. Don't they know we know we're in the midst of this?"

I climb on the bed beside her.

"Hmm, you smell good," she says.

"Verbena shampoo and lavender body lotion." I rest my head on the pillow and sink into the mattress. I should call my mom, let Dad know I'm fine, find out how Hila is doing. But I'm afraid that if I hear their voices, I'll lose it. I follow Lily's example and try and relax. "Now this part I could get used to."

Lily hoots. "We could all get used to this part."

She carefully rests on the pillow, fanning her hair to the side. She's touched up her makeup and put more gel in her hair. With her eyes closed, she takes deep breaths, and watching her like this, I can't help but see a vulnerability hidden under the layers of mascara and liner.

"I got you something," I say, noticing that she's brought my backpack in from the car.

She sits up. "I love presents."

I pull out a bag of jelly beans and hand it to her.

"*Yummy*," she says, taking the bag from my hand. She rips it open and turns it upside down on the bed. Quickly, she sorts them into color piles and slides the licorice ones over to my side.

We munch the beans and watch the end of *The Sound of Music*.

"Climb every mountain," Lily croons. "Till you find your dream." Lily looks at me. "The blondie does it better."

"Julie Andrews? She's had more practice." I lay back. "Hey Lily." I pause.

She lifts one of her sculptured eyebrows. "What's with the face? You look like you just swallowed a lemon."

"I was really scared out there before. I hate myself for panicking. But it makes me wonder, you know?"

She scoops up some red jelly beans and pops them in her mouth. "About . . . ?"

"About everything. Last month all I wanted was to get into a combat unit, be on the front lines, be where the action was, but maybe I—" I pause, it's so hard for me to admit it. "Maybe I misjudged myself. I don't have that tough outer shell like you do."

"Tough outer shell? You make me sound like a walnut."

"I mean, the kind of armor rockets bounce off." I can't

look at her, so I stare at the TV screen. "I'm scared. I don't want to feel that pounding fear inside my chest ever again." It's on the tip of my tongue to say, 'I want to go home,' when I remember that Lily's house has been bombed and she has no home to run back to.

She nods. The coconut jelly beans and the lime ones are the only two flavors left.

"Suppose," she says, "that these here coconut jelly beans represent the kind of guys who go for girls like you."

"Nutty?"

"I'm working on something hypothetical here." She scowls at me.

"Okay."

"And these here green ones are the kind of guys who like booty-licious girls like me."

"Booty-licious?"

"Full-bodied. But what if I want one of these?" she says, popping a coconut bean in her mouth. "I mean, by letting them decide, I give them the power over me, you know what I mean?"

I reach for a lime jelly bean and Lily swats my hand. "Mine," she says.

"I'm having a hard time following your analogy. When did we start talking about guys?"

"I'm talking about control. Jeez. You've got a one-track mind."

"Run that by me again?"

"It's all about control. You can let fear decide things for you. It's always there, always in us. It wants control, but it can only have control if you let it."

As she leans back, I scoop a handful of lime jelly beans into my palm and pop them in my mouth. "Mine," I say.

"You got it, Sugarpear," she says. "Now get dressed because I don't want to be late for the party."

"You still want me to come?"

"What kind of stupid question is that? After I went to all that trouble to find you the perfect dress?"

My eye catches a suspicious object draped across the chair. It is a shocking green Lycra tube with two little mounds rising near the top.

"Tell me that's not the dress you found for me." I groan.

Lily hoots. "Isn't it great? And I've got shoes to go with it. Petite, right?"

I nod, speechless. I have never worn anything green. Never worn anything *that* green in my whole life. I'd argue, but I know there is no point. It was that or the clothes I'd come in, which smelled like goat and fear.

"No, no, Lily," I say, shimming into it. "This isn't me."

"Sure it is. Show them what you've got, that's what I say."

"And that's easy for you to say, you've got it!"

The mirror throws back a reflection of me that would make even my grandmother blush. The green sleeve clings to me, accentuating my hips and every other rise and fall I wasn't even aware I had. My hair is wet and falls in soft curls below my shoulders. Lily pencils on black eyeliner around my eyes and hands me some lip gloss.

"Aggie, you've got more than you think you have. Trust me."

"I do," I say, holding her gaze, realizing that I trust Lily completely, trust her instinct, trust her friendship, trust her every intention. "I do trust you, but—"

She laughs. "Come on. It's getting late."

I'm not sure if it is getting late for the party or we've been above ground for too long and that it's time for another rocket launch. My stomach still has the jitters. I don't want to waste time asking, so I follow Lily out of the hotel and down the stairs toward the shelter.

But I stop before we reach the door and put my hand on Lily's shoulder. "I don't feel right."

"You look great," she says, fiddling with the scoop of her dress.

"No, not that. I don't feel right going to a party and dancing now."

Lily's smile fades. "You don't want to go to my cousin's wedding?"

"It's not like that. I'm really happy for your cousin, but it's the timing."

"My mom and my aunt have been waiting a long time for Rita to get married, so don't tell me about timing."

I look down. Lily knows what I mean. "But with all of our soldiers . . . ," I whisper. "The rockets falling, people injured and killed, it just doesn't feel right."

Lily straightens up and sticks her face so close to mine, I can count her eyebrow hairs.

"Aggie, please. This is so important to me. I need you there with me."

It's dark where we stand in the musty stairway going down to the bomb shelter. Her breath is warm and smells of jelly beans. I don't have to see her well. I hear the catch in her voice and know that her mascara is probably making mud slides down her cheeks.

"Oh, Aggie." She sighs. "You know we're never supposed to put off a wedding to wait for a time when there's peace or life is looking up." Lily takes a deep breath. "Sometimes it just doesn't get better. We have to do this now."

Reaching up, I wipe away the dark smudges from under her eyes with the back of my thumb.

"*Ken*, Commander," I answer.

"Good." Her bottom lip turns out to an exaggerated pout. "So you'll stay?"

I wrap my arms around her and hold her tight. Her body shudders with each breath. I squeeze her tighter. "It's going to be the best wedding ever."

We stay wrapped in each other's arms, trying to recharge ourselves.

"Sometimes it's hard to know what's the right thing to do," she says, her voice coming in jumpy blurts.

I wait a beat. "That's when you need to use your instinct."

We giggle.

Taking a deep breath, she pushes me back, and I see her roll her shoulders, stick out her chest, and put the Lily face back on.

"Ready?"

"After you."

And we make our entrance. The prewedding reception is in full swing. Lily's presence seems to make the musicians play louder, the atmosphere get bouncier, and the crowd more boisterous.

"This baby is mine," says a tall guy with broad shoulders and dark black hair.

"Avi! When did you get here?"

"Right now. I've got twenty-four hours' leave, and I don't plan to waste a second of it." He scoops her into his arms. I can't stop smiling at how happy she looks.

"I think we should have the ceremony now while it's quiet out there," Rita's mother announces.

"Outside?" I turn to Lily. "Why not down here?"

"Rita wants a traditional wedding ceremony outside under the stars with only a chuppah covering her." Lily shrugs. "What Rita wants, she gets."

The chuppah holders grab the canopy and race up the stairs and outside. The bride almost jogs under the chuppah and around the groom. The rabbi runs through the blessings. They sip the wine, on goes the ring, the marriage contract, more wine, the groom smashes the glass, and before we can finish shouting "Mazal Tov" we're racing back to the bomb shelter, relieved that we made it through without an air raid siren going off in the middle.

I dance with all the men in the room. Twice. Which is not so much since the number of women greatly outnumber the men. I think of Noah moving to the music. Long and lanky but graceful. I imagine him holding me as we sway to our own rhythm.

Between dances, Lily's mother tries to stuff me with every dish they've brought. I've eaten enough spicy food to start a brush fire.

"Lily, do you think it's safe to go up?"

"Why? You need some air, or is my mother driving you crazy?"

"A bit of both, and also I promised Roy at the hospital that I'd bring him some wedding cake."

Lily's mouth drops open. "Are you crazy? You're not going out there on your own again!"

"But I promised. It doesn't seem fair not to come through because I don't have the courage to drive a few meters."

Lily's got a love glow in her cheeks. "Hang on," she says, pulling out her cell phone. "I'll call the local security center and see if you can tag along on their next patrol." She waves to Avi, who's talking to her mother. "You sure you want to leave now? Things are just heating up."

The party is showing no signs of winding down. The bride's mother is fanning herself into a frenzy and the dancers don't stop, they just change partners. I nod my head. "I'm only going for an hour."

I wait while Lily calls and explains the situation.

"Okay. Army escort service is ready and waiting," says Lily.

I breathe a sigh of relief. "Thanks. I wasn't so keen about taking to the road on my own again."

Lily gives me a hug. "But you would have anyway."

I push her away. "Where am I going to sleep tonight when I get back?"

She shrugs. "Don't worry. I'll find you a place." And she blows me a kiss. "Say hi to Roy for me."

The mothers at the dessert table hear where I'm going and pile me high with cakes and treats. I don't know how I'll carry it all.

"And give some to the soldiers."

"Of course."

Outside the bomb shelter the silence hits me like a sudden windstorm that sweeps away everything in its path. A burnt smell lingers in the air, signs of another rocket that must have fallen somewhere in the vicinity. I carry the stuff to the car and put half on the front seat and save the other half for the soldiers in the army carrier. I consider changing, but my clothes are in the hotel and I'm too frightened to go inside by myself.

I've done this trip once before. Made it there. And back. I can handle it. Sure, I've been knocked down. But I got up. And now am ready to race forward again. Ready for whatever comes my way.

Chapter Nineteen

"Food," says one of the soldiers, relieving me of the plates as I reach the army carrier. "Smells great."

"So does she," says another soldier.

I smile and roll my eyes as they become more interested in getting my phone number than the plates of food I've brought. I make it back to Lily's car and slide in behind the wheel.

The driver keeps to the speed limit. We reach the traffic light and he stops. I pull up behind him. The soldiers in the back wave and blow me kisses. I wave back but am glad we're all in our separate vehicles. Driving is a breeze now. Much easier than the stomach-clenching trip I made earlier.

But once we pass the light, their guy starts to speed up. I

give a little more gas. He goes faster. I don't like this game of tag. I don't want to be left behind again on my own. Lily's car doesn't hug the road like an army car, and as I speed up, my tires spin on the asphalt.

I'm cursing them under my breath and thinking of all the things I'm going to say to them when I get there, when a strange sound distracts me. It's a humming, a buzzing that's getting louder. I lift my foot from the gas, hoping it's not something that I'll need to stop and fix. But the noise isn't coming from under me. It's coming from above. I glance up.

Helicopters!

I can't see them yet. It's too dark. But the drone is impossible not to recognize.

My body stiffens. They seem to be following me. Helicopters heading toward the hospital. It can mean only one thing: they are bringing in the wounded. I let the army carrier race on ahead, realizing that they have been signaled to come and help out. Their speed has nothing to do with me. They've forgotten all about me in their urgency to get to the landing pad as the choppers arrive.

I shift into fifth, floor the gas, and speed into the hospital lot. I skid into a half-hour parking zone, and I get out. The sky has become a hive of activity. Some choppers are circling above; others pass by, headed farther south.

I force open the steel door to the underground shelter, step in, and shove it closed tightly behind me, blocking out the noise. Juggling the plates of treats, I fight to compose myself as I find my way to the ward.

"Cake," I announce as I walk in, a smile plastered to my face.

"Aggie!" shouts Roy. "You came back."

"I said I would."

Like a swarm of hungry bees, the kids surround me in seconds. The head nurse comes to my rescue with paper plates, napkins, and forks.

"Vanilla icing," says Roy. "My favorite." He helps himself to a huge piece of cake and gives me a vanilla smile.

I divide the marzipan roses between them.

We devour the cake while trying to ignore the commotion in the corridor that's growing louder.

"What's going on?" I whisper to the nurse.

"Something big," she says. "Many wounded."

"Where?"

She answers quietly. The name has a familiar ring.

"Most of the wounded are being flown to Haifa," she says, reaching over to wipe smudges of icing off the chin of one of the kids. "We don't have the staff to deal with more than the lightly to moderately injured."

My insides shrink, trying to imagine what that means.

She sighs and stands up, rubbing a cramp at the small of her back, arching her pregnant belly forward.

"Are you all right?"

"Just finding it hard to breathe," she says.

"Me too," I say.

She squeezes my hand reassuringly. "They'll need some help in Emergency. We're so understaffed."

"Maybe I can do something?"

"I'm sure they'd appreciate it. Find the nurses' station and ask there." She looks at me. "There's a smock behind my desk. Put it on. You don't want to get that nice dress dirty."

Leaving the children's ward, I weave my way around the bustle of doctors, nurses, and patients crowding the corridor. There is a buzz of activity around me.

I glance into the rooms. If Noah is here, that means he is wounded. If he isn't here—it could mean something much worse.

An orderly struggling with a stack of sheets and blankets calls me over. He dumps them in my arms. "Take these to the rooms at the end of the corridor. We need to have more beds ready. Quick. Move."

I hike the load high in my arms, locking my chin on to the top of the pile so it won't tip over. Reaching the last room, I dump everything on the first bed, help the nurse make up the other beds, and head back for another load.

After five runs, my back aches. My arms throb from the strain. But I don't stop. There are rooms that still need to be readied, and the staff is expecting me to do it.

Someone puts a cup of tea in my hand and tells me to drink up. It's too sweet, too weak, and lukewarm. Disgusting. I gulp it down.

"Take these." The orderly who had me hauling blankets and bedsheets now hands me two trays off a food trolley. "Room one hundred and six. The two first beds. When you're done, move on."

I rush between rooms. Give out the trays of food. Collect the empty ones. Have no time to stop and breathe.

"We need someone to watch over the switchboard," one of the nurses calls. "You," she says, pointing to me. "I'll show you what to do."

She explains that I am to take messages from the parents and promise friends and loved ones that someone will get back to them soon. "It's not easy," she warns. But my voice is calm, efficient, and sympathetic. The nurse listens and nods in approval. I ask if I can slip in a call to my sister and leave a message on her phone that I'm fine, helping out in the hospital, and for her to call Mom and Dad and tell them not to worry.

"I'll be back as fast as I can," says the nurse.

A list of patients and their room numbers is dropped before me.

I pour myself another cup of tea and drink it down without tasting it.

The nurse from the children's ward comes in. "How are things?" she asks, resting her hand on my shoulder.

"I know one of the soldiers," I say, pointing to the paper on the desk. I drop my head in my arms, feeling the wall of resolve inside me beginning to crumble.

She pulls me to my feet. "Then what are you doing sitting here? Go. I'll cover the switchboard. You have a more important job to do. Go on. And take off that stained smock."

"But I look—"

"Gorgeous," she says, smiling.

Without giving myself time to lose my nerve, I walk toward the emergency room. The room I've been avoiding.

I pause by the doorway. He's talking to Jonas. I recognize Jonas's long sandy hair beneath his cap and the sling around his shoulder. He's standing by the bed. I lean against the doorjamb, catching snatches of their conversation.

Noah's voice sounds broken. ". . . snapped at him about his boots. He never cleaned his boots right. Always smudged at the heels. Never shaved close enough either."

I hear him choke up.

"Death is beyond our control," says Jonas. His voice is soft as he struggles to keep it steady.

Noah gives a slight shrug and turns away. "I just wish I could have—" His voice catches.

"But you couldn't have known. You can't blame yourself."

"No. But now all I can think about are all the stupid things I said to him. I can't even hear his voice anymore. Just hear myself barking at him." His voice cracks.

I squeeze my hands into fists, the nails biting into my palms. I peek around the corner. Jonas has turned aside, giving me a full view. Noah stares past me.

I can't move. I can't. I can't go in there. The din of the hospital fades into the background. There are no other wards, no other wounded. There is only Noah. I gulp a huge breath, trying to push down the lump of fear.

"So, you know at the beach?" says Noah, his voice sounding faraway.

I strain to listen. His tone has changed.

"The beach?" says Jonas, sounding confused.

"Yeah. You know when you're at the beach and it's the end of the day?"

"Which beach?" says Jonas. "Tel Aviv?"

"Whatever. Tel Aviv, Nahariya. A beach. And then the sun, it starts to sink, and as the last bit of light is about to disappear, suddenly there's this green light in the sky?"

"A green flash," says Jonas. "It's one of those rare natural wonders."

"A phenomenon," says Noah.

"So what about it?"

"I think I just saw one."

There's a pause. "Must be the drugs," he says as he turns to follow Noah's gaze.

Then noticing me, Jonas smiles. "Oh, *that* green flash." He nods and moves away from Noah's bedside. "Okay, Noah, I'm going to see how the other guys are doing. You sure you'll be okay?"

"I think so. Wish I had my guitar, though. See if you can find one for me, later?"

"Sure."

Jonas pauses beside me before leaving. "I'm glad to see

you," he says. Our eyes meet for a second, and I see that his are brimming with tears.

I take a step into the room. Noah watches me.

"Interesting uniform," he says, nodding his head in approval. "I like it. Is that what the women combat soldiers are wearing these days?"

"In your dreams."

"That's true." He doesn't take his eyes off me. "Most combat units for girls are in the canine corps training the dogs. First one I've heard that involves lost kittens."

"Has Jonas told you everything?" He's teasing me. I try laughing, but it sounds feeble even to my ears. His gaze is penetrating and I glance away, but not without noticing how thin his face has become.

"It's good to see you," he says. "I'd get up and hug you, but my leg—" He pauses.

No one's trained me for what to say next and no words rush to my rescue. "How bad—"

"I'll be all right"—he cuts me off—"which is more than I can say for some of the others."

I take a few more tentative steps in. I can see he's straining to get a whole look of me—all the way down to the green spiky shoes. I let his gaze linger.

I make it to the side of his bed. He reaches out. I run

my fingers down the length of his arm. He turns his hand palm up. His long, delicate guitar fingers swallow my hand in his. I notice the shell burn marks on his inner arm and can't stop myself from flinching.

Wiggling my fingers, I weave them through his. His hand feels steady, strong, and cool. We look at the way our fingers intertwine. It's easier than looking at each other.

Somewhere in the corridor a medicine trolley wheels by. The generator pulses, making the lights flicker. A voice calls out for a nurse. Noah rests his head against the pillow, staring at the ceiling.

Suddenly, overwhelmed, my voice cracks, "Oh, Noah," I say.

"What?" he asks softly.

I shake my head.

"Talk to me, Aggie."

"It's so much harder than I ever imagined."

He waits for me to go on.

"I thought I could do it. Signed up for combat. Aced boot camp. Came up here on my own. Drove through a war zone. Dodged a rocket. Raced helicopters." The words tumble out of me. "Lily said you've got to control your emotions. But the fear. The strain of fighting for control. The stress of wanting to be everywhere at once. I—I know

I thought I could. But seeing you here—like this." I shake my head. "I can't. I'm not cut out for this."

"For what?"

"This." I gesture with my free hand. "You were right. It takes a certain type. And I don't think I have it. I've been holding it all in. Doing what I have to. But inside," I say, putting my hand to my heart, "inside I can't anymore."

He squeezes my hand. "I don't think you understood me—"

"No, I didn't then. I do now. I'm not cut out for this. I'm not brave enough."

Our fingers are still intertwined. I try and pull my hand away, but he doesn't let go. We're silent for a few minutes. I wish I could absorb the pain that he is going through, make it easier, but know that's impossible, too.

"So what made you come up here in the first place?" he asks. "Shouldn't you be home?"

"My parents think so. But I came because . . ." I pause, thinking back to what seems like a million years ago. "Lily called me. Her house was totaled by a rocket. I couldn't sit at home and leave her to deal with it on her own, not after what we'd been through together." I look at him pleadingly, hoping he won't think the worse of me. "But now all I want to do is run away and be someplace else."

Which at this point isn't really true. I don't want to be anywhere else except here, beside him.

"Wouldn't we all?" he says, conviction lacking in his tone. "But we are where we are, and we have to make the most of it."

He eases his grip, as if to let me free. But now I squeeze his hand harder. I sink into the chair by the bed and drop my head into my hands. I haven't cried. I'm not going to. I'm not.

We stay quiet for a while, our fingers entwined, inseparable. He hums the refrain of the song "Darkenu," singing softly, "But you won't walk alone. I'll be there with you."

I think I understand what he means. Seeing Noah and Jonas together, different in so many ways but connected. It's a bond of brothers not less than the one between me and Hila or the one I've made with Lily. Had I thought it brave going north to be with Lily? Bravery had nothing to do with it. Lily had everything to do with it.

Finally I raise my head. Noah is still watching me. His eyes are softer, tender, slightly teasing.

"And just so as you know, I never had any doubt that you weren't the type—or my type."

"You're teasing, and I'm too tired to come up with a

witty quip." And as if by admitting to the exhaustion, a wave of weariness washes over me.

"Where are you planning on sleeping tonight?" he asks.

I shrug. "Don't know. Lily said she'd find me a place when I got back. I should call her."

Noah sucks in a painful breath of air. He raises himself higher. I jump up ready to call the nurse for help, but all he's done is shift himself to one side of the bed.

"It's not the best or most private accommodation," he says, his dimples betraying any hint of humility, "and certainly not the way I imagined our first night together. But if you want to join me—"

"You can't be serious. Here?" I glance over my shoulder. "With you?" My voice catches in my throat.

"Well, sure. What about it? People are always holding out for the 'perfect time.'" He slides his hand down the empty side of the bed. "But really, the perfect time is when you turn the present into what you want it to be."

I'm reminded of Lily and the wedding and Avi and find myself blushing.

"Look, Aggie. It's finally just the two of us. Shira's not here to drag you off somewhere. I'm certainly not going anywhere." His gaze coasts over me. "And you"—he takes a breath—"are wearing that incredible dress. What better timing than this?"

Totally embarrassed but totally convinced, I kick off the spikes and sit down on the bed. He watches, smiling, and raises an arm to make a place for me beside him. I lay down, resting my head in the nape of his neck. My body fits right next to his. His arm circles around my shoulder, drawing me closer.

"I'm sure this is against the rules," I say.

"Not worse than running a red light."

"What? Is there anything you don't know?"

"About you? Plenty—at least a thousand things." He nuzzles the crown of my head with his scruffy chin.

I tilt my head up to smile at him. He caresses my cheek, gently lifts my chin, and bends until his lips touch mine, and we kiss.

Chapter Twenty

A monitor starts beeping; a voice crackles over an intercom. I open my eyes to find Noah's mother leaning over him on the other side of the bed.

"Mom," he says. "Wow, you got here fast."

"Fast? To me it felt like forever." She gives him a kiss. Resting a hand on his forehead, as if trusting her touch more than any thermometer, she heaves a sigh of relief. "What do the doctors say? Are they taking care of you?"

Noah laughs and runs his hand down my side. "No complaints," he says.

I sit up, wishing I could slip away unnoticed. Dalia's face looks strained and creased in places where her smiles used to be. She is holding Noah's hand, and the tears sliding down her cheeks are all she allows herself. She doesn't speak anymore. Doesn't utter a sound. Her shoulders shake silently as she struggles for control.

"I'll be fine, Mom. Really."

She nods her head. Takes a deep breath. Exhales.

I slip off the bed and start inching toward the door.

"Abigail."

"Yes?" I turn around.

"Please, don't leave."

"I'm not leaving. I just thought I'd . . ."

She clears her throat. "Wait. I have a message for you. There's an army transport leaving here for Jerusalem. I promised your mother I'd make sure you were on it. Stay here with Noah. I'll tell the driver I've found you and you'll be joining them."

She walks out of the room, chin up. I can tell that she needs a reason to leave and compose herself, though I know she's also giving Noah and me a few more moments alone. I run back to him.

"I don't want to go," I say.

He reaches up to smooth down a curl that springs back. "Stubborn," he says, tugging on a strand. "But still, you're no match against my mom. You need to go back home. Your parents must be worried."

"I want to stay here with you."

"I may get a few days off." He looks away from me and brushes his palm across his forehead. "But if the doctors say I'm fit and my unit is going back in, if I can, I need to be with them."

As I open my mouth to object, he pulls me closer and places his lips gently by my ear. His breath is warm, intimate, sending tremors down my spine. "It's just how things are, Aggie. It's complicated, but I think you can understand. Anyway, one thing I know for sure, as soon as I get home, I'll want you with me every second." His lips linger by my ear. "And you'll be there, right?"

I nod my head, too undone to answer.

"Take my jacket. You're a danger walking around like that."

I'm not sure how I manage to pull myself away, but I find myself swaddled in Noah's army jacket, his mother's arm around me leading me to an army bus, where she tucks me into a seat by the window.

"Thank you," Dalia says as she kisses the top of my head. "Thank you for being there with Noah." She takes a deep breath. "I'm sorry you'll miss Shira. She's on her way up with her father."

I cover my hands over my face and groan.

"What's wrong, dear?"

"I haven't told Shira yet about me and Noah," I say, cringing with embarrassment.

Dalia laughs. "And you're telling me she hasn't noticed how my Noah acts around you?" She strokes my head. "Okay. I promise I won't say anything until you tell her."

"Thank you." I slump back against the seat. "Now I have to face my parents. They're really mad at me, aren't they?"

"They're worried, of course. But they're also very proud of you."

"Really?" I stare up at her.

"Really. They told me all about how you're determined to get into a combat unit. They said, 'When our Aggie puts her mind to something, nothing stands in her way.'"

"I wish I could call them. Tell them I'm okay. Tell them I'm sorry for worrying them. But I've left my cell phone and all my stuff in the hotel room and now it's too late to pick them up."

"Here, take my phone." She hands it to me. "I don't need it."

"Oh no, I couldn't. There must be so many people who want to call you, see how you are, how Noah is—"

She shakes her head. "And that's exactly why I don't want it on me. I need some quiet time. Make your phone calls and then turn it off. I'm sure you could also use a few minutes to yourself."

I take the phone and slip it into the pocket of Noah's jacket. "Thank you."

"I'll get Shira to pick up your things—though I'm sure you'll be back soon enough." She gives me a knowing smile and leaves.

The bus fills up slowly with soldiers and civilians. A girl sits down next to me. I scrunch closer to the window, tilting my body away from her. I can feel her eyes peering at me curiously. I must be an odd sight in an army coat, short skirt, and high-heeled shoes.

"Nice outfit," she says, laughing.

"Yes, I know. I look ridiculous."

She sticks a bag of chips in front of me. "Want some?"

"Thanks," I say. Taking a few, I realize how hungry I am. I give her a grateful smile.

She looks me over. "You don't recognize me, do you?"

She's wearing high-heeled summer sandals, tight jeans, and a black sleeveless shirt. She smells slightly like Amber Romance, a scent I recognize because Hila bought me some for my last birthday.

"You look really familiar," I say, "but I'm sorry. My brain isn't working."

She laughs with a light kind of carefree lilt.

I take a closer look. I know I know her. But I'm

stumped. Her hair is cut short and feathers softly over her ears. Green eyes, bright and candid, look at me teasingly. There's something about her that is so familiar, but I draw a blank.

"I always get a kick out of it when this happens," she says.

Leaning back into my seat, hugging Noah's coat around me, I'm torn between wanting my solitude and a nagging curiosity. "Were you in one of my classes or something?"

She slaps her thigh and laughs louder. "You spend an intensive period with someone, and you'd think you'd leave more of an impression, but I guess not."

"Okay," I say. "Give me a hint."

She clears her throat. Sits up and turns to me. Her jaw tightens. Her eyes narrow. Her posture stiffens. "Forty seconds. That hill. To the top! Back! Now!"

My mouth drops open. "*Ken!* Commander. Forgive me. I didn't recognize you." My spine becomes ramrod straight.

She slumps back and laughs. "Relax, Number Eighteen. We're both off duty." She runs her hand through her hair. "What's your name again? I'm great with numbers but names . . ."

"Aggie."

"Right! Abigail Jacobs."

"Tami," she says, reintroducing herself. "But I thought you were a Jerusalemite. What are you doing all the way up here?"

I tell her about Lily's house being hit and the animals and helping out at the hospital.

"Why do I think you're leaving out the best part?"

I squirm. "Must be the oversized army coat."

She smiles. "Of course. A dead giveaway. I've got one, too." She sighs. We both let our heads loll against the seat. The bus speeds down the deserted highway as dawn spreads across the horizon.

"What are you doing up here?" I ask.

"I got a few days off to help my parents. They've got a hatchery up past Nahariya, and all their help has been deployed." She giggles. "But it wasn't all chickens and eggs," she confesses quietly. "Yesterday I got to spend the afternoon with my boyfriend."

She's got such a silly grin that I can't help but laugh, too. She crosses her legs. "So you came all the way up from Jerusalem to be with Lily." She offers me more chips. "I knew you two stars would hit it off," she says.

"Stars?" I say, unable to keep the disbelief out of my voice.

I think of what I'm going to tell Lily, and my head is

racing with questions. Tami picks up a chip, pops it in her mouth, and licks the salt off her fingers. Turning to face me, she gives me one of her commander looks, a look I recognize. I steady myself and wait.

"You still have a long way to go, Aggie. There's basic training, which is tough, a lot tougher than the little sample you had." She cracks a smile. "But then, if, after two years, you are where I believe you'll be, you and your sidekick Lily will be leading a group of new recruits."

"Just like you?"

She laughs. "Why not? You certainly have what it takes."

I want to ask her more, but just then her cell phone starts crooning a soppy love song. She glances at the number on her phone, motioning me to wait while she takes the call.

"Hey, love," she says. Her voice drops to a whisper, and she shifts slightly to the other side. I turn back to the window to give her privacy.

I'm wiped. Exhausted. Done in. Tuckered out. My body droops from the strain of it all, except for a slight smile I feel lifting the corners of my mouth.

I slip out the cell phone from Noah's jacket and dial home. "Hey, it's me. I'm on the way back home. But listen, I've got some great news!"

Epilogue

I am about to jump.

I am about to jump wearing a full load on my back.

Feet, knees, hip, back, roll.

Crammed tightly, the pack is stuffed with my anxieties, fears—and the army-issued parachute. It is secured to my chest with strings and clasps. It holds my heart in place, should it try to break free. When the time is right, I will yank the cord.

At that moment, the pack will open. My fears will rise to the dome of my chute, where they will hover. And for a moment, I will be free of them.

Feet, knees, hip, back, roll. I have been trained to react without thinking. My body knows the drill. I will fall. Drift. Soar. Once my feet make contact with the ground, I will drop to my knees, lean into my hip, flip onto my back, and roll.

Not another rehearsal; this is reality. Am I ready? Yes. I can do this. Really, I can.

The door is pushed open. A rush of air blasts at me. The noise of the airplane motor swells and crashes inside my head.

I am sandwiched in. We shuffle forward like penguins. Birds without wings forced to fly. My hands clench the rungs. I have been trained for this moment, but nothing can tame the terror in my bones and the fear churning in my stomach.

"Green!"

I'm not ready to let go.

"Jump!"

The air batters against my chest, pressing me back. The engine thunders in my head.

And then my fingers are pried from the rungs.

There are moments in life when you have to jump. You throw yourself into the atmosphere hoping you'll land right, hoping your parachute will open and ease your fall. If you're lucky, you'll have a crowd of onlookers waiting on the ground to greet you. Some chutes glide with the wind until you land effortlessly. Others get caught up in turbulence and the ride down to earth is bumpier, the landing harder. The thing is you never know how it'll be until you step out and take the chance.

And when you hit the air, before your automatic parachute opens, there are a few seconds in which you are suspended. Skydivers call it freefall. I like to think of this time as that fleeting moment in life when you can see everything with unusual clarity.

As I peer out at the land rising up toward me, I am amazed at how small it all looks, as if I can scoop up all the land and cradle it in the palm of my hand. I wonder, as I am watched from below, if I look like a kite that has broken loose from the strings that once held it.

Feet, knees, hip, back, roll.

The ground is hard: *feet.*

The impact quick: *knees.*

But I am quicker: *hips.*

The sky retreats: *back.*

I am home: *roll.*